Two Steps Forward

Read more about Annabel in

The Steps

Also by Rachel Cohn

Shrimp
Pop Princess
Gingerbread

Annabel's Family Tree

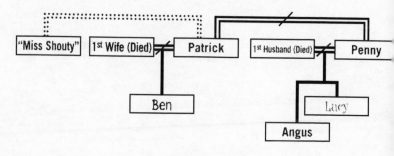

"Miss Shouty" — 1st Wife (Died) — Patrick — 1st Husband (Died) — Penny

Ben

Lucy

Angus

Two Steps Forward

Rachel Cohn

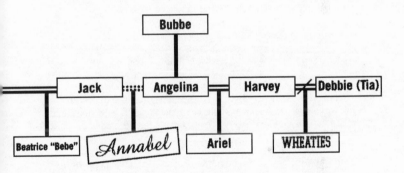

Simon & Schuster Books for Young Readers

NEW YORK • LONDON • TORONTO • SYDNEY

i

SIMON & SCHUSTER BOOKS FOR YOUNG READERS
An imprint of Simon & Schuster Children's Publishing Division
1230 Avenue of the Americas, New York, New York 10020

This book is a work of fiction. Any references to historical events, real people, or real locales are used fictitiously. Other names, characters, places, and incidents are products of the author's imagination, and any resemblance to actual events or locales or persons, living or dead, is entirely coincidental.

SIMON & SCHUSTER BOOKS FOR YOUNG READERS is a trademark of Simon & Schuster, Inc.
Book design by Michael Nagin
The text for this book is set in Aldine 721.
Manufactured in the United States of America
2 4 6 8 10 9 7 5 3 1
Library of Congress Cataloging-in-Publication Data
Cohn, Rachel.
Two steps forward / Rachel Cohn.— 1st ed.
p. cm.
Sequel to: The steps.
Summary: Fourteen-year-old Annabel's extended family gathers in Los Angeles for several weeks over the summer where she must contend with step- and half sisters and brothers and her own mother's failing marriage.
ISBN: 978-1-4424-9615-6
[1. Stepfamilies—Fiction. 2. Remarriage—Fiction. 3. Family problems—Fiction.] I. Title.
PZ7.C6665TW 2006
[Fie]—dc22   2004025681

For Monica and Violet

ଔ

Acknowledgments

With thanks to David Gale, Alexandra Cooper, "Team Jennifer," Alicia Gordon, Joe Monti, and Svett Strickland

Chapter 1

Annabel

Bubbe says I should try to take five deep breaths before I snap at my mom. Bubbe would know. She had years of practice raising my mother and learning how impossible Angelina could be.

"Annabel, you're sulking again," Angelina said. My mother was actually trying to put on lipstick while the baby squirmed in her lap and the plane bumped through turbulence.

One . . . two . . . three . . .

"Am NOT!" I snapped, even though I was. I grabbed my baby half sister from Angelina's lap and kissed the baby's soft, warm head. Pretty soon Ariel's little head is going to look like a prune from all the times I use it to shut my mouth when it wants to lash out at our mother.

Better to sulk than all out fight, I suppose. My mom

and I hardly ever used to fight but now "GO AWAY!" and "How dare you speak to me in that tone?" are like the foundation of half our conversations. She says it's because of my teenage hormones, which it's NOT. *She* is the problem, not me. *She* starts the fights with me, just like she starts them with Harvey, my stepdad. Angelina has so many fights with him that now we're on our way from New York to Los Angeles to spend the summer away from him, to give Harvey and Angelina "space," as she says. Like they've tried so hard on "together" before needing "space." They've been married barely a year.

Angelina reached for the floor and lifted my purse—a sweet little Prada knockoff from Canal Street, ten dollars after bargaining the guy down from fifteen, thank you very much. She unzipped the purse and was about to put her hand inside it, right in front of me!

"Don't touch my bag!" I snapped, again. I grabbed my purse and placed the baby back on Angelina's lap to keep my mother's hands busy and off my stuff. I mean, I can't believe she did that right in front of me. Does she not know a fourteen-year-old girl's purse/backpack/EVERYTHING is sacred space, completely off-limits to the mother species?

Angelina shook her head. Her shiny honey-colored tresses, the pride of so many shampoo commercials, fell perfectly into line along her shoulders. "Oh, teen moody girl, so sorry. I just wanted a compact mirror to put on my lipstick. Relax. It's not like I was looking for your diary or anything."

"I don't keep a diary!" God, how uncool does she think I am, anyway? Diaries: how *common*.

Angelina pointed out the window, like she could distract me from my rising fury. "Look, the Rocky Mountains. Won't be long till Los Angeles now, Annabel baby."

La-la land. So-la-what! I wanted Sydney, Australia. That's where I was supposed to be spending my summer.

When I stared at the seat ahead of me instead of looking out the window, Angelina said, "I don't get the sullen face. Your father and I went to extraordinary effort so you could have a summer with him and his family. I thought Lucy had been upgraded from unwanted stepsister to your best friend. Last summer you couldn't wait to be on the plane to spend vacation with her."

Last summer Lucy and my other family lived in Sydney.

Last summer was winter in Sydney, but in that upside-down world, my other family—my other life—worked great, with no need for a location change. Sydney was where Jack, my dad, had that elusive thing called a "stable marriage" with Lucy's mom, Penny, who I didn't like at first on account of her kidnapping my dad across the world and all, but now I like her fine. She is totally in love with my dad and I have to respect Penny's good taste. I just would have liked visiting Penny and all The Steps that came along with her better in her native country, Australia, in my adopted other-home city.

I miss you already, Sydney! That city has cast some kind of spell on me. It's like New York is my first love, but I will totally cheat on it for Sydney. It has to be the most beautiful city I've ever been to. New York is obviously the most exciting and important city ever, but it's all skyscrapers and pulsing energy and grunge, where Sydney is light and lush, with beaches and vistas, great weather and—weirdness—friendly people. And *hello*, shopping! New York has the fashion mecca of "the four *B*s" as I call them—Bloomingdale's, Bergdorf, Barneys, and Bendel—but since I'm on a highly unfair and measly allowance, I'm lucky to afford a fake designer bag on Canal Street. I bet there is no good place to shop in LA that does not involve skinny socialites or teen starlets whose fashion trends I most certainly will not be following anytime soon.

Why did the parental units have to ruin everything by deciding to move the base of family operations to Los Angeles? At New Year's, Jack and The Steps moved to LA for Jack's career—he's a talent manager who represents some successful, and apparently getting much more successful, Australian comedians—and to be closer to me. Then Angelina decided we should spend the summer in LA because she might have acting opportunities there, and also, Wheaties, Harvey's son, goes to LA in the summers to stay with his real mom. My mom adores her stepson; she just didn't want his father, her husband, as part of the LA package.

The only thing to look forward to about getting to LA would be the quality of the airport greeting from Lucy. The louder and more embarrassing, the better. My stepsister and I like to one-up each other with airport greetings in front of swarms of people, preferably using loud, inappropriate drinking songs we learned from the Internet.

Last summer when I arrived in Sydney, Lucy was waiting for me outside customs, but what I saw first was the sign attached to her feet, which were about shoulder level to my dad, standing next to her: HEY ANNABEL, WE'RE RIGHT HERE! Lucy's head was close to the floor, her mouth grinning at me from the bottom of her handstand.

Lucy is like the upside-down, Australian-sister representation of me. She even wears the same size, so we can share clothes. Two wardrobes are always better than one, even if my clothes taste is more advanced than hers, although . . . grr . . . some tees look more advanced on her than me as Lucy's got more "boozies," as our toddler sister Beatrice has learned to say. That's what Australian people do for some reason, cut off words and end them in "ie," which is how "bosom" becomes "boozies" (at least in The Steps' Aussie vocab) or "kindergarten" becomes "kindie," or whatev-ie.

But what I lack in the boozies department, I more than make up for in fashion sense, and since Lucy has no vision when it comes to putting outfits together and accessorizing, I am there to fill that gap for her. We balance each other out somehow, like she's the other half of me. I would just like my half of the boozies, please. Anytime now, God, anytime.

I was trying to figure out how Lucy would be waiting for me at the airport this time around—would there be a costume, some form of glittery signage, or maybe a live band like I got for her when she came to visit me in NYC?—but Angelina forgot about my sulk and dove into chatter mode, probably from the two coffees she'd consumed since takeoff from JFK. My mom is just one talkathon person; she cannot respect a good trance that's trying to tune her out. That's why she always gets cast in commercials for communications equipment like cell phones and long-distance services, because she is incapable of just being quiet. "I've got two auditions already lined up in LA! Ever since the Fresh4U commercials started airing, my agent's been getting a ton of calls. Maybe LA will be my big break, baby! Maybe I'll break free from commercials already and land a pilot or a feature! I've always thought if I could just spend more time in LA, I could get the work I want." She squeezed my hand and I decided to be nice and squeeze back, just a little. Angelina's so pretty and, much as it pains me to admit, she is basically a very nice mom when she's not being nosy. It's hard not to occasionally fall under her spell, even when I am monster annoyed with her.

The Fresh4U commercials. Oh, yes, the reason why I can't show my face at my new school next fall, ever. I'm starting ninth grade at a posh girls school in Manhattan where Angelina also went to high school. It's like a rich-mean-girls school, but only the smart ones. The school was definitely not my first choice, but with Angelina and Harvey having so many problems the last year, I didn't want Angelina worrying about my high school choice, too. It was easier to agree to go to her alma mater, where we knew I would get in, than to put us all through the application process for a bigger range of schools. But as if the having to wear a uniform, the NO BOYS factor, and the not knowing anyone at this notorious den of snobby girls doesn't make me dread the approach of September enough, lucky Annabel also gets to start her new school as the legacy daughter of the new spokeswoman for a new brand of feminine products called Fresh4U. YAY, wave cheer!

Feel your freshest self. The commercials air every minute on every channel in the universe. I hear my mother's voice saying that in my sleep now. What does that mean, anyway, *Feel your freshest self?* I don't even want to think about it. My big fashion statement next year at my new high school will probably be the paper bag I'll be wearing over my head. Maybe I'll slap a Gucci logo on the paper bag so all the snob-girls at my school will think I'm leading some new, designer-label fashion trend. PAPER BAG, by Annabel Schubert, for Gucci.

Maybe LA isn't such a bad idea, after all. Maybe I can apply for asylum and live permanently with my dad and The Steps. Jack and Penny hardly ever fight—in fact, when they're not dealing with kids kids kids, they're usually making out, which is soooo gross, but also sort of sweet. And it could be cool to live with Lucy and go to school with her, and to be around to watch baby Beatrice grow up. If I was there in person, I could mold Beatrice's fashion tastes from a young age, and she could become like my perfect-style protégé. I've tried with Lucy, and it just is not going to happen. If I lived with them, my other stepbro, Angus, and I could make our shared fave mac and cheese dinner together every night, because we are the vegetarians in the family. Angus would keep me honest, because he is much more serious about it than me. I mean, I love animals—who doesn't?—but I also love chicken cacciatore, even if I try not to eat it. Angus loves fish more than anything and knows more facts about creatures that live in water than probably the whole marine biology department at Sydney University does. Don't ever order a Filet-O'-You-Know-What if you're at Mickey Ds with Angus or you will see one major screaming fit. Which I totally respect.

But there's also something funky about staying with Jack and The Steps. Like it's all fun, but it's a vacation. It's real life, but not really, because in real life, I have a mom who makes rules, I have my own bedroom, and I have my own life with my own friends back in Manhattan. I always know that no matter how much fun I have with The Steps, I will be leaving again.

I know that Angelina is scared that I could possibly one day ask to live with the other family permanently, because every time I returned from visiting them in Australia she would sing me this terrible rap she made up: "Sydney and Dad/are not so bad/but remember/there's no better place to be/than in NYC/with me me me!" She must have sensed that I was fantasizing about living with them as I stared out the plane window to LA, trying to ignore her, because suddenly Angelina sang out, "Ben!" dropping the word she knows can sidetrack me from mad to glad in an instant. And I admit, for a moment, I fell for it; I stopped thinking about stupid LA and *feel your freshest self* because I was sighing and picturing Lucy's former stepbro and the crush of my life, Ben, and let's pause for a moment of silence at the mention of his name and breathe in, out, *Ben Ben Ben* like yoga people go *om om om*.

Even though hearing his name could instantly conjure an image in my head of his tight footy god calves and his beautiful face of green eyes and rumpled mess of brown hair, I was not going to let Angelina manipulate me into a happy mood so easily. I met Ben my first time in Australia, a year and a half ago; he was my first kiss and all, but it's not like we've kept up our little romance after all this time and across so much distance between New York, where I live, and Melbourne, where he lives. (Lucky Melbourne!) And if Angelina knew anything about true love instead of about ruining love relationships, her specialty, she would know not to tease me about him.

So I asked Angelina, "Aren't you worried that we've abandoned Wheaties?" because I think she should feel very guilty about separating us from Harvey's son, even if Wheaties is a dork. But he's our dork.

Wheaties and I went to the same school until the end of this last term. We're the reason our parents even met. He has a real name—Alan, or Al—but everyone at school called him Wheaties because he's a scrawny, brainy boy who's got to be the last person you'd ever see pictured on the cereal box draped in sports medals. Our class was big into irony during seventh and eighth grades. Wheaties kind of grows on you, though. I almost wish he could come to that all-girls school with me in the fall.

Angelina snapped back, "You know perfectly well that Al's arriving in LA not long after we are so he can spend the summer with his mother and that, of course, we will be seeing a lot of him! And I *don't* appreciate your tone, Annabel. LA is going to be great, with or without your attitude problem." She put on the movie headphones so now she could ignore me. She is so deluded.

Seriously—what could LA offer that could beat Sydney? Other than the hope that somehow during a summer away from New York and Harvey, Angelina's Fresh4U commercials might stop airing before I start high school in the fall?

I did appreciate that Angelina's LA plans meant I will be close to Jack and especially to Lucy, but at the same time, the whole idea of spending a summer in LA, away from Harvey and with no idea what, or who, we will be going back to, filled me with dread. Bubbe says being filled with dread is part of my family heritage from her side, along with knowing not to wear stockings with open-toed sandals or blue jeans to the ballet at Lincoln Center.

When our plane landed at LAX, all I could think was: Lucy, please have a great airport scene planned to cheer me up and take away this dread. I knew my girl Luce would come through for me. But as Angelina and I emerged from the arrival area with the baby in a stroller and a ton of luggage, we were greeted by . . . NOBODY! I asked Angelina, "Where are they?" thinking maybe Angus would suddenly sprout from hiding beneath a potted plant or Lucy would round the corner wearing a white balloon outfit and aiming a paintball shooter. Angelina said, like it was nothing, "Oh, didn't I tell you? Penny offered to pick us up, but I'm renting a car from the airport so I told them not to bother." Thanks for consulting me first, Mom, thanks a lot.

Breathe breathe breathe Ben Ben Ben oh love of my life; who cares about Sydney or even LA? I wish I was spending the summer in AUSTRALIA with YOU, where it's winter and I could wear great sweaters and snuggle close to you like in a Ralph Lauren ad and not think at all about this stupid summer my mom has planned, all because her marriage is a disaster.

From the rental-car window, LA looked like an alien universe. The baby must have known our new city was all wrong, because she started screaming in the car as we drove through the traffic-mobbed, palm-treed streets, with what felt like a layer of brown smog covering our car. YUCK.

I hate LA.

Chapter 2

Lucy

I love LA.

Sydney was miserable, and Melbourne, where I grew up and from where I was snatched when my mum married Jack, is the best, of course, but I am completely on board with the LA experience. Mum, not so much. She doesn't appreciate the perfect weather and the perfect people who all look like supermodels, or that you can randomly be standing in line at Starbucks behind Reese Witherspoon, the way I do.

"Penny," I said, "aren't you sick of watching footy on the telly yet?" In Australia we had to beg my mother to allow our household to have a TV, and now she not only insisted we have a wide-screen TV in our new house, but she made Dad get premium satellite service with stations playing Aussie sports, and worse,

Aussie soaps. She never watched *Neighbours* when we lived in Australia, but now it's like the world is over if she misses it!

I gently tried to take the TV remote clicker from her tight grip. She sat on the couch but in some weird yoga pose, her feet on the sofa cushions, knees bent, arms hugging her knees. I pointed at the telly and reminded her, "This is a prerecorded show. We already know who won this game. Not only are you watching an old game, but you're watching a rerun of an old game. Penny, are you listening?"

My mother stared at me with the deer-in-the-headlight look she's had ever since we moved to Los Angeles. "Lucy," she said. "I am your mother, not your friend. We are not Angelina and Annabel. I answer to 'Mum,' not 'Penny.' And don't think you're an American now and should call me 'Mom.'" Mum—not Penny and not Mom—said that last word, *Mom*, with an exaggerated American accent that sounded like she was blowing her nose while saying it.

"*Mum*, will Dad be home soon?" I looked at my watch, worried that Dad wouldn't get back from his office in time for Annabel and Angelina's arrival at our house. If Dad wasn't here to greet Annabel, who knew what direction that could shift her mood? She'd blame me or Angus, for sure, even though the real reason Dad stayed late at the office, I suspect, is to dodge Angelina. I don't know how Jack and Angelina were ever a couple. They pretend at getting along when we

14

kids are around, but I think they really work each other's last nerve. Dad never yells at anyone, he is always Mister Calm, but when he thinks we're all asleep, I've heard him yelling at Angelina on the phone, words like "inconsiderate" and proclamations like "She's my daughter too—I'd appreciate you discussing these things with me first before making these decisions."

"I don't know when he'll get home," Mum said, but I could tell she did know and was trying to be tactful. "He's got Angus with him at the office now. I think he and Angus are having their boy time. You know, some last moments before the summer female invasion hits."

Great. That means Annabel the Moody when she comes over. I am totally "stoked," as the surfie boys here say, that Annabel is spending the summer near us, but that girl is way moody. The funny thing is, she thinks it's everyone else that has the problem, not her. I love Miss New York Attitude, I really do, but if she for a second thinks that Jack is favoring our family over her, it's like time has to stop until she can get over it. And, he never favors us over her. That's her paranoia.

Ooh, *paranoia*, good word. I ran to my room for my diary. I like to look up words in the dictionary and then write about that word in the diary. "*Paranoia*. What Dad feels about Angelina spending the summer not just in the same city as us, but only a few blocks away! The house Angelina is renting this summer is so close, we can even walk there, and as Mum and Dad always sing, ♪ *Nobody walks in LA.* ♪ Then they start laughing and kissing (again) and it's really gross, and me and Angus still don't know what's so hilarious about nobody walking in LA? Am I *paranoid* for wondering?"

The doorbell rang, which must have woke the baby from her nap, because as so often happens in our house, the rare moment of peace and quiet instantly changed to a variation of NOISE-yell-NOISE-thump-NOISE-ring. Beatrice whined, "Mummy!" from her crib; Mummy yelled, "Luce darling, can you answer the door?" followed by the sound of her feet scuffling to the baby's room; and impatient Annabel (I'm sure) hit the doorbell like a thousand times.

I rushed to the door, happy to see Annabel at last! Count on my stepsister to be fully fashioned out for a travel day. When our family made the long journey to LA from Sydney, we all wore track suits and sneakers and grumpy faces. But Annabel stood at our door, fresh from the plane, grinning and wearing crisp designer jeans (she irons them! she really does!) with high-heeled boots and a fitted white tee that said DIVA in sparkly letters. She was so cute, too, wearing the infamous cowboy hat she got her first time in Sydney—the "dreadful hat" as I used to call it, with the letter *A* stenciled on the front and beads dangling down from the rim.

I let out a little scream, "AHHH!" because that's what I do when I'm glad to see someone. I can't help it. I gave Annabel a quick hug because I couldn't wait to take Ariel, Angelina's baby, from her. Now that our sister Beatrice is toddling all over the place and talking up a storm, it's nice to have a replacement baby, especially one so pretty and who hasn't yet learned to wail "NO!" or to give herself a nickname like "Bebe" because she can't yet pronounce her own name. Angelina's baby is almost as gorgeous as Angelina. I know you're not supposed to love a baby just for having big blue eyes, rosy red pinch-able cheeks, and a mat of white-blond fairy hair, but Baby A could definitely be the Ivory soap beauty baby. I don't know how Harvey ever agreed to let Ariel be gone from him for a whole summer.

Angelina said, "Oh my, just look at you, Lucy!" Her smile was as big as Annabel's frown. "Developing quite the figure, aren't you?" Annabel crossed her arms over her chest, and I'm fairly sure my face turned red. That's such an American thing, commenting on bodies like that in front of a person.

I hope when I grow up I have a figure like Angelina's. Actually, I want to *be* Angelina, except for the failed relationships and drama-queen antics. She named her new baby after a recurring character she played on a soap once—how cool is *that*? Angelina has promised to give me acting lessons this summer, as I plan to one day be the world's first surfing-champion

Oscar-winning actress, in exchange for surfing lessons.

I led the *A* girls inside the house. Annabel said, "No party going on inside? No band about to play?" She looked around more and said, "Hey, where's the boy?"

Annabel's not used to having an arrival that does not involve Angus running over to her like some desperate puppy. In a casual *no big deal* voice, I said, "Dad and Angus are at Dad's office. They should be back soon." I knew I needed to distract Annabel from the fact of their absence, and luckily I had one big surprise stored up for her. I set Ariel down on the floor to crawl back over to Angelina. In a *yes, big deal!* voice, I added, "GUESS WHO'S COMING HERE SOON!"

"Not Dad," Annabel said, in full sulk mode. "Clearly." She plopped onto the sofa. Uh-oh, here we go.

"BEN!" I screamed, and the surprise worked like a Lucky Charm, my new favorite American cereal that Dad lets us eat on mornings when Mum sleeps in late and can't whine about bad American foods ruining our health. Mum's obviously never tasted Lucky Charms cereal. Poor dear, she has no idea what she's missing.

The "Ben" word turned Annabel's sulk right around. "GET OUT!" she said. Mum came into the room carrying Bebe, whose head was on Mum's chest, her big pretty eyes with the long black eyelashes sort of half opened. Annabel grabbed my hand instead of checking out how much our sister had grown in the months since she'd last seen her. "Where's your room? You have to tell me EVERYTHING. Hey, Penny. Hi, Beatrice." Annabel didn't try to kiss Bebe because she knows Bebe has to get used to Annabel all over again before she'll accept kisses. Annabel will also have to get used to calling our sister "Bebe" because Beatrice's name for herself seems to be sticking.

We left the mums and their babies in the living room. I couldn't wait to show Annabel my room—*our* room. In Sydney, she shared my room, and my new room has bunk beds set up for when Annabel will stay with us. I hope she will stay with us a lot even though Angelina's house is nearby. Sometimes I hope Annabel could live with us permanently, even if she is a diva. I never feel sad or lonely when Annabel is with us. Probably because I'm too entertained guessing her moods.

Annabel jumped onto the bottom bunk and fingered the linens. "Are these sheets percale? Because Bubbe says percale sheets aren't always top quality."

I don't even know what *percale* is. I marked the word in my head for a future diary entry. That Bubbe knows a lot about stuff. Although Dad says that Bubbe's pronouncements are as often wrong as they are right. Dad says Bubbe just *sounds* like she knows what she's talking about. But Annabel told me Dad and

Angelina's mum never got along anyway, so I don't know whose opinion to trust.

Annabel didn't notice that I had a picture of Leonardo taped on the wall on the bottom bunk—just for her, because she'll probably still love him when he's playing someone's grandpa in a movie. She also didn't seem to notice that the pink curtains matched the mauve carpet that picked up the white and yellow flower-patterned linens nicely. Mum and I had spent hours at Target choosing colors that would match so we wouldn't have to hear Annabel comment about clashing palette effect, whatever that is.

Annabel dropped the linens from her fingers. "BEN!" she said. "What's the deal?" I knew the magic word could turn her mood around.

"Mum got an e-mail from Patrick last week," I told her. Patrick is Ben's dad and Mum's ex-husband, though it hardly seems that way because they weren't married even a year. They met in a support group for people who'd lost their spouses and had young children. According to my gran, Patrick and Mum got married because they were lonely, but they really didn't love each other except as friends. "Patrick has a new girlfriend, and it sounds like it's getting serious! Imagine that, Ben with a new stepmum, maybe. This lady has always wanted to visit America, so Patrick saved up his money and they're all coming here during Ben's school hols."

As we say back in Oz, Ben is a spunk—totally cute

to the extreme—but I never crushed on him like Annabel, or even much noticed him that way until Annabel noticed what a hot guy he'd turned into from the shy boy I remembered from when my mum and his dad were married. Annabel can have him—I mean, he was my brother for a while there! Also, he's a good bloke, but his sportiness and hotness have turned him into a popularity magnet, too, which I find to be an uninteresting combination in a crush target. If I wanted a boyfriend like Annabel does, and I don't, but if I did, I reckon I would fancy a weird guy who was arty and depressed rather than popular and dreamy looking.

Annabel lay on the bed and kicked her legs up in a bicycling motion. "YES!" she exclaimed. "Ben Ben Ben! I knew you would take away my dread."

"What dread?" I wanted to know.

We spent the late afternoon in our room, with the door closed and the mums not bothering us. We had so much to catch up on, and Annabel's dread to talk about. I told her about how moving to LA had been like a Get Out of Jail Free card for me. In Sydney, I didn't have many friends because I was always the weird girl from Melbourne, but in LA, being the girl from Australia gave me unexpected coolness—and the kids here love my Australian accent. Go figure! The harder part to figure out is why sometimes when kids hear my accent, they either talk back to me really slow and loud, like I couldn't possibly understand them, or else when I pronounce certain words (like "great") they repeat it back to me using a bad Aussie accent (so it comes out like "graayate").

Annabel pulled a book from her cute handbag to show me. The book was about some clique of horrible, mean girls at a posh school like the one Annabel is going to in the fall. "Read this and you'll understand why I am wishing high school would never start," she said. What I love about Annabel is that on the surface she can seem like one of those posh-school "snob-girls," as Annabel calls them, but when you get to know her, you could not ask for a sweeter person. Annabel is like a fancy manicure in a deep red color that's too mature for the person wearing it but there's no nail polish remover to be found: it just takes a little work to scrape down the sophisticated varnish.

Angus burst into our room right as Annabel was telling me about her other stepbrother, Wheaties, and how his mum lives in LA and now he's coming to LA this summer too. Angus jumped right onto Annabel's lap as an almost-seven-year-old will do. "What did you bring me?" he asked her.

We have this ritual gift exchange we go through every time we see one another after a long time apart. We brought Annabel prezzies from Australia, which we'd been holding on to until we saw her in LA, but I hadn't gotten them out yet because I knew Mum and Dad would want to see her open them.

Annabel smiled. Her smile could light a room; she

should use it more often. "Guess!" she told Angus.

"You promised me some Kinder Surprises," he said.

Annabel pulled up her backpack from the floor and took out a Ziploc bag full of Kinder Surprises, which are chocolate eggs with a toy in the middle, a treat that's popular in Oz and the UK but that we haven't yet figured out where to find in LA. Annabel answered, "And do I ever let you down, Nemo? Angelina and I found this store in Greenwich Village that sells all these Aussie and British foods. I brought Vegemite for your mum. I still think that stuff is totally gross. I don't know how you can spread it on bread like it's butter or jam, but whatever. And I brought proper New York bagels for Dad." Annabel Claus with the prezzies then handed Angus a bag from the American Museum of Natural History filled with fish toys and tossed me a fake designer purse from her favorite street in New York that sells all the cheap knockoffs. The shoulder bag pictured my favorite old-time movie star in my favorite movie, Audrey Hepburn in *Roman Holiday,* with red rhinestones sewn on the tiara part of Audrey's princess picture, and it was filled with bags of Smith's Salt and Vinegar Crisps, potato chips only an Aussie could appreciate, which are about as hard to find here as Kinder Surprises. Oh, beautiful girl Annabel! Love her!

Dad must have picked up the smell of the bagels because almost instantly he was standing at the doorway to our room. For a man with four children, dozens of clients, and no spare time, he always manages to look happy and not tired. Maybe it's because he's so tall and friendly looking. Or maybe it's because he's still in his thirties and isn't ancient like a lot of other dads at my new school in LA, where there's a whole posse of bald-headed guys with paunchy tummies and expensive watches who are becoming grandpas at the same time that their new, younger wives are making them new dads all over again.

Annabel lost all her NY cool at seeing Dad. She ran to him and jumped into his arms, squealing, "JACK!" Her hug looked like it could squeeze the life out of him. Annabel's parents had taught her to call them by their real names when she was a baby, but even though Jack and Angelina have since grown up as much as Annabel and have told her they're okay with "Mom" and "Dad," old habits must die hard, because Annabel still goes back and forth between using their proper names and their parent names.

Angus leaped up from the bottom bunk where he had laid out the fish toys. "Dad, come see . . ." but I grabbed Angus's arm and pulled him back to the bed. I shook my head at Angus and whispered in his ear, "Josephine Snickercross thinks Annabel and Dad need some time for themselves. What different species of fish are these toys? Josephine wants to know."

"Really?" Angus asked, distracted by the mention of Josephine's name. Dad touched Annabel's long hair, and she took his hand. They walked away down the hallway together, deep in conversation.

Josephine Snickercross is a character my real dad made up. She's like Mary Poppins crossed with a sorceress (but a good one) from a Harry Potter book. Mum was pregnant with Angus when our real dad died, so Angus never knew him. But Angus looks so much like our dad that sometimes it makes me want to cry, and sometimes it makes me want to smother him in hugs except for how Angus often reeks of smelly socks. My real dad was the greatest man ever, and since Angus is the closest person to me connected to my dad, I make it my mission to make sure Angus knows our real father through me. If Angus is all into water creatures the way our marine biologist father was, well, who do you think gave Angus his first goldfish? And it was me who gave Angus his six hundred-plus page favorite book of photos and facts that's become like his personal encyclopedia, *Aquarium Fishes of the World.* I have sadly lived to regret that one. He wants The Book read to him all the time, and it is torture to read for anyone who is not 100 percent fish-obsessed, which is like everybody except my real dad and Angus.

According to our father's made-up stories, Josephine Snickercross descended from a long line of secret Tasmanian mermaid royalty, and she only came on land to take care of and teach magic to certain children specially chosen by destiny, because mostly she'd prefer to hang out in the sea with all the other mermaids. Dropping Josephine's name never fails to get Angus to do what I want him to do—in this case, leave Annabel and her dad alone for a little while.

For Angus and me, Josephine Snickercross is like a genie in a bottle of memories that only I can open.

Chapter 3

Annabel

Blunnies: shoe stylings only Australians could come up with and only a New Yorker could make chic. I may wear my ultraplain new Blunnie boots with my stupid school uniform next fall to kick-start a revolution against the hordes of expensive-designer-shoe-wearing upper-class girls. People, fashion FORWARD.

I stood in front of the full-length mirror on the closet door of my new temporary bedroom, modeling the gift Blunnies that Jack, Penny, and The Steps brought me from Australia. *Blunnies* is short for "Blundstone" (that Aussie "ie" thing again), and they are workman-style ankle boots with elastic strips along the sides, probably the most boring looking shoes ever, but somehow, because of their everyman-ness, the most interesting boots too. They can be worn with anything—jeans, khakis, even skirts—and manage to look cool. Blunnies are this random but crucial Aussie export like Kylie Minogue that if you try to understand the popularity, your brain will explode from confusion, so better to just go with it.

Should I go for a Kylie look when I see Ben? No, too much makeup, and archy eyebrow work required— tacky. Let's see, I could wear the brown Blunnies with a basic Gap tan skirt, and I'll borrow one of Lucy's Aussie footy shirts, the one for the team (I think it's Essendon) that wears the black and red colors, two colors I normally wouldn't put together, but in this ensemble it could work. I can wear my hair long and curly, with some sprayed-on red streaks to pick up the red of the footy jersey. A simple, smart look, but funky. Ben is all jock, so I'll wear one of those loose jerseys and maybe that will help him not notice my lack of cleavage underneath.

Lucy says I am boy-crazy. She says that like it's a bad thing. I don't know why she's not more boy-crazy. The girl has gotten so pretty since I first met her, with curvy hips and chest and long, lean, tanned surfer legs, yet she seems not to care whether boys notice her. She says she likes boys as friends first, and when the time and the boy is right, she will want to date one, but she's not in any rush. How very sensible of her. And BORING! Lucy's a Nicole Kidman waiting to happen, I suspect. Nicole was like this regular Sheila (as those Aussies might say), then she married Tom Cruise and became a nice wife and mum but never a big movie star. Then after Tom dumped her, she changed—blossomed. Makeover city: she straightened and lightened the hair, got herself some ultraglam gowns, and those Oscar roles poured in. Sorry now, Tom? It was like Nicole didn't know anything was wrong before, but when things changed—wow, could she do any better? Lucy is a budding Nicole for sure, not waiting around for a Tom (Lucy has better taste), but once she gets discovered, watch out.

I could hear Angelina on the phone in the living room, arguing with someone. She had to be talking to either Harvey or Bubbe. I almost liked hearing her cross voice because it reminded me of home. Our apartment in New York bustles with people and noises and random shouting matches. Even though I am less than happy about this LA thing, maybe the arguing has gotten old, and maybe this spooky-quiet canyon scene will help Angelina figure things out.

Our summer rental is a single-level, plain old 1950s ranch house perched up in a very steep, woody canyon between the Hollywood Hills and some mythic place called "The Valley." The house is spooky in this very boring way. The hardwood floors are dark, and the whole house seems to absorb that darkness because the windows are surrounded by trees and hardly any direct sun shines in. The furniture is strictly Ikea, and there's no artwork or pictures or anything on the walls to spice up the look. I'm sure this house was possibly haunted in the past, but then the ghosts left because they were too bored whimpering around a house this dull. In Manhattan, we live in an old limestone apartment building with sooty gargoyles perched on the exterior landings, so we can rest assured that quality haunting is going on there.

The quiet here creeps me out, but maybe that's because the scary creatures are waiting for late night to make noise. Supposedly there are like coyotes and snakes hanging around up in the canyon. Are you going to go outside in a real city like NYC or Tokyo and stumble on that kind of wild life? No, I don't think so.

If I need some familiar noise and chaos, I can walk down the hill to Jack and Penny's house (love that I can do that, still hate being in LA), but I've only just gotten here, and sometimes I forget after I haven't seen them for a long time how awkward it is to readjust to The Steps. I don't think it's fair that every time I see them again after a few months apart, I have to get used to their family rhythm all over again. For once I would like them to have to re-acclimate to ME, instead of me to them. Like, Beatrice—sorry, it's Bebe now, apparently—should remember me and come running for me to pick her up instead of needing us to reacquaint all over again before she can be comfortable with me like a proper sister. And you know who really bugs me? Whoever Josephine Snickercross is— some mysterious lady that Lucy and Angus talk about in hushed tones together. I could just ask them who

Madame Josephine is, but I am determined to find out on my own, and also, I don't want them to know I am that interested in someone who is their little private secret.

Here's my private little secret. Back in Australia, Ben was my first real kiss—and it's a year and a half later and I still haven't gotten another one! Now that I'm starting an all-girls school in the fall, my chances are rapidly dwindling. I have to make this summer count.

Ben Ben Ben. Maybe it's a long time since I've seen him or even e-mailed with him—long distance relationships are hard, it turns out, especially given our different time zones and different sides of the equator — but I have my trusty little Ben box handy at all times to remember him by. I swear I'm not some stalker freak.

I reached under the bed for the Ben box that I'd stashed as soon as we had arrived at this house. The Ben files are treasured inside an old, aluminum construction-worker lunch box I found at a flea market in Sydney, and it's filled with photos of him, some articles they ran about him in the sports page of his neighborhood newspaper because he's practically famous in his little hood for what a great footy player he is, and printouts of e-mails and IM sessions we had together in the few months after we met in Australia. Eventually we just stopped talking via computer. Sometimes you need to see an actual person instead of a screen name to keep up a relationship that's more than a crush. So even though Ben was my first kiss, all the time and distance between us has bumped him from virtual boyfriend back to just plain crush, but I have the Ben box to always remember him by. And pretty soon, I'll have the real thing!

Om om om.

I sat on the bed and looked at the last class photo of him that Lucy's best friend from Melbourne, who goes to the same school as Ben, sent to Lucy for me. He had the same brown hair but it was no longer short, now more a mess of wavy strands falling to just below his ears. His hair was almost a girly style but worked because Ben has such an angular guy face, with intense green eyes and a slightly crooked nose from being broken too many times playing rough sports. I would say his whole look now is very David Beckham: masculine sporty dude, but in touch with his feminine-hair side, too, and not ashamed of it.

Australian football is so way hotter than any other sport, in my opinion. It's like this mixture of English rugby and American football, with the drama and obsessive fans of international soccer. The players don't wear helmets or padding and there are no time-outs, so watching Aussie-rules footy is like seeing a fast and furious gladiator rumble of extremely muscular, sweaty guys.

When he's finished high school, I bet Ben will realize his dream to become a professional footy player, being cheered on by a stadium full of "supporters," as they say in Oz. And of course Ben's number one supporter will always be there: me, his loving wife. I'll be Posh to his Becks, Down-Under style, with maybe a whole sideline career for us starring in commercials for like cool Japanese gadgets and gizmos but never personal-care, Fresh4U-type products, obviously. As an added bonus, Ben and I will be too busy being the perfect couple to even notice potential crush distractions, so our union won't be troubled by the usual tabloid scandals.

I stared at the photo of Ben Ben Ben so intently I didn't notice Angelina had come into my room until she bounced onto the mattress next to me. She took the photo from my fingers. "Ben again!" she said. "Do we need to have that certain special talk now that Ben's coming to LA? You know, the birds and the bees . . ."

I placed my hands over my ears and wailed, "AHHHH!" I mean really, we have premium digital cable service at our apartment in Manhattan. Does Angelina think I haven't seen the late night movies on Cinemax? God, how embarrassing.

Also, *birds and bees*! Whoever made up that expression should definitely be placed under citizen's arrest. Luckily I could play Angelina's game as well as her, and I knew just the name to drop to throw her off this awful trail.

I took my hands down from my ears and asked, "Was that Bubbe you were talking to on the phone? Why don't we invite her to come visit us here?"

Angelina twirled a strand of my hair. She loves to do that. "Yes it was, and why don't we not?" Sometimes I suspect the reason Mom was in such a rush to marry Harvey had more to do with her wanting to be independent of Bubbe than with Angelina wanting a real future with Harvey. Acting is a really hard career to make a living at, and Angelina is lucky because she does get jobs, but she's never had acting work steady enough to support us living on our own in Manhattan. And my mother doesn't do Brooklyn or Queens. So after a few years of us living with Bubbe after Angelina and Jack split up, my mother, I think, wanted to be independent of Bubbe telling her what to do all the time, like: get a regular job, grow up. Bubbe said listening to her wisdom was the price Angelina had to pay for being an adult with a child living in her mother's apartment. I guess that price was too high because Angelina only dated Harvey a few months before deciding to plunge into marriage and new parenthood (again).

Angelina stretched out sideways on my bed. She pulled me down next to her and nuzzled her face into my neck from behind me. I resisted the urge to squirm out of her embrace, because I'm all about the relaxed *om* vibe right now, and also, she felt warm and cozy in this cold house. Angelina said, "I am so happy to be gone from New York! I forgot how much I love LA. Maybe it's time I considered going back to school, finish my degree I started at UCLA so long ago—what do you think about that idea?" Mom smoothed down my hair. I'm the reason she dropped out of college between freshman and sophomore year of college. She'd met Jack when they both had summer jobs at a restaurant in Manhattan. The rest is history.

What I think about that idea is it's a great one—so long as she plans to go back to college in New York and not keep us here in LA past this summer.

"Bubbe would like it here!" I mumbled. Bubbe probably *wouldn't* like it here, but Annabel would like Bubbe being here, and that's usually reason enough for Bubbe.

Angelina said, "Bubbe would not like it here and you know it! She doesn't even know how to drive, and do you really think she could survive more than a week being outside a ten block radius of Zabar's? And in a house where smoking is forbidden?" Angelina pointed to the little sign on the nightstand that said THANK YOU FOR NOT SMOKING. Nice homey touch, right?

"Do you miss Harvey?" I asked Angelina. Because I felt like I needed to know. I'm not going to worry about missing Bubbe. She has a way of showing up whether she's invited or not, usually wearing a great tweed suit and some old-timey handbag on her arm, with a cig dangling from her mouth. It's a not-so-original, classic granny-chic look, but it works on her.

"Haven't been gone long enough to miss him," Mom said. "And he's lost to the business transaction right now, so even if we were home, we wouldn't be seeing him. Why else do you think he agreed to let Al spend the whole summer here with his mother instead of just the usual three weeks? Harvey knows he can't be the family man he professes to want to be until he gets that albatross of a business unloaded." Harvey owns a chain of mattress stores across the tristate area, but he's been in negotiations to sell the business to a larger chain for the past few months. It's true we haven't seen much of him since the negotiations started. Mostly we hear him in his study shouting "UNACCEPTABLE TERMS!" into the phone.

If I were a shrink, not the frumpy kind, but like a lady psychiatrist from the movies—young and sexy, perhaps with the unfortunate problem of a crazy patient trying to kill me, but I get to wear great couture clothes from Barney's—here's what I would speculate: While Angelina possibly married Harvey to break free from Bubbe, then Harvey married Angelina so his son would have a family, and then Harvey wouldn't have to worry about the fact that he and Wheaties' real mom share the same affliction—workaholic-itis. But while this shrink may have a diagnosis for why Angelina and Harvey's marriage went wrong, she does not know the cure to make things all better again.

It's hard to believe that just over a year ago we celebrated Harvey and Angelina's marriage. Harvey and Angelina had a brief ceremony in the back garden of this French restaurant in the West Village where they went on their first date. It was a beautiful wedding, really. The walls of the garden were strung with vines of white flowers: roses, calla lilies, gardenias—it smelled like paradise back there. I got to be maid of honor in a dress I designed myself, and Wheaties was his dad's best man, and Bubbe cried and cried, but the good kind of crying. Angelina never looked more beautiful than in her ivory Chanel suit that covered up the bump that was baby Ariel, and the yarmulke on Harvey's head perfectly covered up his bald spot. I don't think it was my imagination that Harvey and Angelina genuinely looked happy and excited. The food was delicious even if it did make me belch a lot, and they had cupcakes with little bride and groom figures on each one instead of having a huge cake—a nice touch, I thought. During the reception, a little jazz band played in the garden, and Wheaties and I danced all night even though at school we would never let on we could get along so well since we were in totally different friend groups.

I thought newlyweds were supposed to be all blissful. Jack and Penny were—and still are, even though they have a baby, Lucy and Angus from Penny's first marriage, and me from Jack's previous relationship, plus moving their family to the other side of the world. How come Harvey and Angelina couldn't be 100 percent sure that they even wanted to be married to each other, before they had to make Wheaties and me be in a whole new family again?

I don't know what makes a "normal" family, but one thing I do know is that when I'm older, I'm going to fall in love and get married just once, for keeps. Hopefully I will marry Ben, and I'll be wearing a supremely fabulous dress of course—I'm loving on Badgley Mischka right now, and Ben will look awesome in an Armani tux—and we won't wake up in a daze a year later and be like, I need some space, man, you're whacking out my whole vibe. Ben and I will be solid, like Jack and Penny. We won't need time-outs, because we'll be playing the whole game straight through, Aussie footy style.

Chapter 4

Lucy

We've lived in LA for six months and I'm still adjusting to the change in seasons. In July in Australia, we're in winter, with short, brisk days and long, cold nights, and lots of schoolwork. Here in LA, it's light until after Angus and Bebe's bedtime, the weather is very hot and dry, and school is out until September! I'm so happy Annabel is here, because I don't know how I'd survive this whole winter—I mean summer—alone.

All my friends from my new school in LA went away to summer camp or to their grandparents. While I'd love to pass the days at Venice Beach, surfing or rollerblading and generally soaking in the rays, the beach is far from our house, and Mum is still afraid to drive on the right-hand side of the road. When Dad is away at work, the best we can get out of Mum for rides is the occasional trip to the supermarket or to the nearby YMCA. If not for Annabel's arrival, I would be trapped all day with just Angus for entertainment. Which would work for like two hours, and then we'd kill each other.

Even though there is a bed for her in my room, Annabel hasn't once said when she plans—or even wants—to stay at our house with us, which I think means she's undecided about how she feels about being in LA, even though we spent the last few months e-mailing about how excited we were to spend the winter together—I mean SUMMER (Lucy, WAKE UP!). So this morning I've decided to initiate Phase I of my plan to make Annabel love Los Angeles. Who knows, maybe she will come to like it so much she could eventually live with us, and then she would never have to go to that snob-girl school in Manhattan? Or maybe Angelina will land a role on a TV show, and they'll have no choice but to move here permanently? Hopefully Angelina will make sure I get a job as an extra on her TV show, but then the camera will keep panning on my face and the director will be like, "Good God, who is that brilliant girl the camera just can't steer away from? Come here, lass, you need your own show on the Disney Channel! Clearly!"

Phase I of my plan is to introduce Annabel to morning hikes. I am not a morning person like her. I like to sleep at least until ten on nonschool days, but that girl wakes up at the crack of dawn, probably because she wants to make sure she doesn't miss anything by sleeping in like normal people. So here it is, SEVEN IN THE BLOODY MORNING, and not only am I awake with teeth cleaned and hair brushed, but I am all dressed for a workout and ready to walk up the hill to Annabel's. She's like a puppy that needs rigorous exercise every day to let out all that energy, so a morning walk is key. Annabel and I used to go walking together in the mornings in Balmain, our neighborhood in Sydney, so if I continue our tradition in LA, that will help Annabel feel more at home here. I know, I'm a genius. I can't help myself!

Once she spends a morning hiking through the canyon, smelling the jasmine and jacaranda, listening to the birds, and being rewarded with the amazing ocean view once we reach the crest of the canyon (if the smog's not too bad—please, smog, COOPERATE!), there's no way Annabel can't fall in love with LA like I have. You know what would be grand? If we could walk by Leonardo and whatever supermodel he's currently enamored of, walking their dogs in the canyon! Hey, it happens! It's yet to happen to me, but I've seen the pix in *Us* magazine, so I know it's possible.

I let Mum and Dad know my morning hike plan the night before, and they said okay so long as Annabel and I stuck to the popular path that has lots of regular morning hikers, and so long as I swore we'd be home by 10 A.M. or they'd call the police. Police! No worries, we'll be home by ten already, and we'll be expecting a hearty breakfast, so don't slack off, Mum!

I tiptoed from my bedroom and slipped our brekkie menu request sheet under Mum and Dad's door. Now that I am an LA girl, I must get with deconstructing the healthy food pyramid, so I asked for pancakes or blueberry muffins for carbs, scrambled eggs would be grand for protein, and why not some freshly squeezed OJ for vitamin C too—THANKS! The menu safely under their door, I tiptoed to the front of the house so as not to wake anybody, and I had unlocked the front door to quietly slip out when I felt a hand grab my wrist. I looked to my side and saw that the hairy hand was attached to a hairier arm coming from a blanketed body lying on the couch situated beside the front door.

"Oi! Where do you think you're going, young lady?" a raspy voice from under the covers demanded.

I whispered at the body on the couch, "Mum and Dad know I'm going out, Maurice." I wondered if they even knew *he* was here this morning? Maurice is Dad's biggest client, an actor and comedian who got so hot in Australia that American producers came calling, and now we're all in America so he can get his big break that will make him an international star instead of just an Aussie celeb. An American television network has ordered a pilot of a TV show for Maurice, which Dad says is like a test show developed around Maurice's comedy act, and if the network likes it, the show might be on the schedule in the next TV season. And if the network doesn't like the show,

Maurice might be on a one-way ticket back to Oz, economy class. Pressure!

But now that Maurice has this big, exciting TV deal and you'd think tons of money rolling in, and his own proper apartment that the network has set him up in temporarily, you know where Maurice prefers to stay? At our house. He has his own house key, so as many mornings as not, we're likely to find him crashed on our couch after he's stumbled here in the middle of the night after a late-night comedy gig. We don't know if he comes here because he's afraid to be alone in this strange country or because Mum stocks Aussie treats for him, like Tim Tam biscuits and Milo chocolate drink that her friends back in Australia send to her.

"It's bloody early!" Maurice grumbled. "You woke me up!"

Excuse me, but sleep in your own bed at your own apartment and this wouldn't be a problem! It's good for Maurice that he's Dad's biggest and most promising client or I would so remind him that he has his own home—elsewhere. He really needs to get a girl-friend, or we'll never be rid of him.

"So go back to bloody sleep!" I informed him. Mum was still sleeping so I could say "bloody" without getting the I Warned You look from her.

A whistle came from under the covers, followed by Maurice's head peeking out, a head all wild with a black mess of frizzy hair—really, he could be the *Simpsons'* Sideshow Bob's Down-Under cousin.

"Aren't you cheeky this morning!" Maurice said.

"Maurice," I whispered, "nobody appreciates a hung-over comedian using words like 'cheeky' first thing in the morning. Now, be a good Maurice and go back to sleep, and we can forget we ever had this encounter."

I stepped outside of the house, knowing he would fall right back asleep and hopefully be gone by the time I got back home with Annabel. *Cheeky,* indeed. I've asked Dad on many occasions why Maurice has to be at our house all the time when he has his own place. Dad says it's okay because he needs to keep an eye on Maurice—make sure Maurice has a proper shower and a shave before showing up at the studio, please, and also, make sure Maurice even shows up at the studio, thanks. Dad says that since now is the time of Maurice's big break, we all need to cut him some slack and make him feel as comfortable as possible.

Once safely out of the house, I breathed in the fresh morning air. I really do love LA, and especially this canyon! But I had barely enjoyed the walk halfway up the block to Annabel's when I heard loud breathing coming from behind me, wheezes so heavy I had to stop and turn around. Maurice! He followed close behind me on the street, wearing Mum's too-tight pink terry cloth bathrobe over his boxer shorts and grubby white T-shirt that showed off a furry mat of black chest hair, and Aussie lambswool slippers on his feet and his Sideshow Bob black mess of hair on full alert. Maurice looked at me like, *What could be possibly be wrong with me being dressed like this outside for all your neighbors to see?* Maurice had better hope no *Us* magazine photographer lurked behind the trees, waiting to snap a grainy "Stars—They're Just Like Us" shot to run in the magazine once Maurice becomes famous in America.

"Taking a morning hike?" he huffed. "I think I'll join you. Now that you've bloody woken me up and I won't be able to fall back asleep."

Maurice suspects everyone in America, and particularly Los Angeles, of being a violent criminal, which had to be the reason he didn't want me to hike on my own. Actually, Maurice is suspicious of just about everyone. Once back in Sydney, Maurice was hanging out on the front porch of our house and saw this boy walking home from school alongside me, and Maurice chased him away with a broomstick! The boy recognized Maurice from telly and thought it was all part of his act, but, um, it wasn't. Maurice said he was a teenage boy once, and if I only knew the filth running through the brain of that boy who was walking alongside me, I would have chased him away with a broomstick too.

I don't need Maurice ruining my social life here in America, too. I informed him, "You smoke a pack of cigarettes a day. You won't make it halfway up the path." I took in a discreet sniff. At least he cleaned his teeth before charging out of the house.

"Is that a challenge?" Maurice asked. "Let's go!" He leaned down like a sprinter taking his mark, but with his snug pink bathrobe and hair chaos falling backward over his head, he looked ridiculous and I couldn't help but laugh. Eh, why not let Maurice come along?

The window blinds were up and the kitchen lights on at Annabel and Angelina's house. From the front yard, I could see Angelina standing at the fridge holding the baby, and Annabel sitting on the kitchen-counter ledge next to them. When Annabel saw me through the window, she waved and jumped off the counter. She appeared at the front door within seconds.

Annabel only noticed me at first, because she jumped right into Angelina-spawn chatterspeak: "Hi! Did you come so we could take a morning hike like we used to? I wanted to call you so bad to see if we could go walking but Mom said it was too early to call to your house so I'm really glad you're here! You must have known . . ." Her words stopped when she must have realized that the sight standing behind me was not an apparition of a hairy Sasquatch dipped in Pepto-Bismol, but in fact, a fashion-disaster freak the likes of which Annabel probably never dreamed possible.

"G'day, mate!" Maurice chirped, and I couldn't help but giggle again, though I doubted Annabel got the joke—no real Aussie ever says that expression except in movies.

Maybe she didn't get the joke, but she must have appreciated that humor was involved because she didn't morph into Frown Girl Annabel. Instead, her face brightened and she answered, "G'day back atcha! I know who you are. Dad told me about you. You're Maurice! Come on in, Maurice. Care for some coffee and a makeover?"

Wow, Annabel made even the almighty Maurice laugh! Impressive.

Maurice walked into the house ahead of me, and from behind his back, Annabel pointed at her watch and mouthed, "What's he doing here this early?" She knows from the days when our dad was a comedian himself that those comedy types keep very late hours. I shrugged in response. Trying to explain Maurice is impossible, so better to just let her experience him.

I'd already seen their summer rental house when Mum and I inspected it for Angelina, before Angelina paid the deposit, so I went right over to the breakfast nook where Angelina sat with Baby A. "Can I have a go?" I asked Angelina. I sat down opposite Angelina and she passed the baby over to me. I cradled Ariel in my arms and placed the bottle in her mouth. It's so nice that Ariel can't shout at me yet like Bebe, "NO! ONLY WANT MUMMY!"

Annabel went to her room to put on her sneaks as Maurice sat down at the table. I introduced Angelina to Maurice but didn't really pay mind to their chatting because I had important cooing to do at Ariel. She's just so scrumptious, and I can tell how when she fixes her big blue eyes on mine and grabs onto my thumb that she remembers me and, possibly, truly adores me. I didn't look up from staring at her until I heard Annabel come back into the room.

"Let's go!" Annabel announced, now dressed in a perfectly coordinated green and white tracksuit with green and white, unscuffed sneakers. I don't know how she does it.

I passed the baby back to Angelina and asked Maurice, "You're sure you're up for this hike, mate?" thinking I was giving him some reverse-psychology challenge to pump him up for our workout (which he desperately needed, may I just say). But Maurice said, "Who said I wanted a hike? I'm wearing bloody slippers in case you didn't notice, Luce! You lured me here on false pretenses! You said Angelina made the best cup of coffee in Los Angeles, and I will not leave this house until I respect her offer to linger here over a good morning brew. Now go on, and next time, just be honest when you lure me out of the house at the crack of dawn, hey? Pick me up on your way back down."

Angelina giggled. I giggled. Annabel frowned. Maurice's bushy-eyebrow-covered brown eyes had the *Could you be more beautiful?* look going at Angelina. Too bad for him and his makeover potential, because any possible friendship he might have gotten started with Annabel was in dangerous territory, I suspected, by the evil eye she shot him.

"Shouldn't you come for a hike with us, Mom?" Annabel decided.

"Oh gosh, no!" Angelina said. "I'm barely awake, and I am a hike-through-Saks kind of girl, not a hike-through-the-canyon one. But you two be careful and have a good workout." She led us to the door and kissed us both on the cheek.

"You're sure?" Annabel said, leaning her head around to check out Maurice one more time.

"Couldn't be more sure, darling." Then Angelina whispered at Annabel, "It's just coffee! Can't I make a new friend?"

Annabel gave Angelina a somewhat downgraded evil eye but said, "I guess so," sounding less than convinced. "Don't forget Wheaties arrives soon, and you promised you would call his mom about setting up a time for him to come over. Yeah, Wheaties—your husband's son!" She said the word *husband* very loud, I'm sure for Maurice to hear.

Annabel closed the door behind us. As we walked up the hill, she took my hand, which she does sometimes when she's tense. I told her, "Maurice might be a crazy person but he's a good guy, really. No worries."

"He needs a stylist," she snapped. She paused our walk as we reached the entrance to the canyon path from the street. "Are there snakes and coyotes in here?"

"Well, this is a wooded area. Of course there's lots of

wildlife! But I've never seen snakes or coyotes. Look at all these morning walkers and their dogs. I don't think the wild animals come out with this many people and pooches around."

"Okay, then." Annabel had to be a little reassured, because she dropped my hand and perked up. "Can you believe I am excited about Wheaties being here? Who would have ever thought?" If I thought Annabel had been a pain about her dad marrying my mum and making us stepsibs, I can only imagine the attitude Wheaties must have gotten from her when his dad married her mum. But Annabel is the queen of makeovers, and that includes herself. Not only did she get over deciding not to like me and Angus before she'd even met us, but apparently she got over the Wheaties thing too, because that boy has practically become her sidekick since their two families moved in together. But he's a boy and a geek, so even though Annabel likes him now as her stepbro, I'm still number one on her step list because I'm her best friend and vice versa.

"Do you think Wheaties might be the ultimate dag?" I asked Annabel. A "dag" is an Australian word that sounds like an insult but really isn't. A daggy person is like a nerd, but funny and sweet, endearing. Annabel and I had a game we made up back in Sydney called Who's Your Favorite Dag?—so in tribute to that tradition, we passed the time on our long hike up the canyon path discussing dags like they were case studies for a school report.

We decided:

Dags have been famous throughout history. Lots of kings who were the result of too many cousins intermarrying and who had inferiority complexes because of their heredity were probably dags—at least the nice ones who didn't kill people randomly for being the wrong religion or something. Annabel saw a TV movie about some American president called Truman who was this scrawny underdog that everyone rubbished on, but now he's considered to have been one of the best American presidents, so she nominated this Truman guy as her country's most famous dag politician. But kings and presidents and famous historical people like that are boring, and why do schools make you do reports on them anyway?

There are two kinds of dags in the all-important teenage-boy category—the hot kind and the not-so-hot kind. Using TV history as a case study, we concluded the best example of the hot kind would be the Seth Cohen character on *The O.C.* Hot dags are goofs and underdogs, but they always win the hot girl in the end. I pointed out several cast members of *Neighbours* who were hot dags, but Annabel said Aussie soap actors are only known in the UK and Oz unless they become breakout international pop stars and we should really only use recognizable TV examples. I offered, Milhouse from *The Simpsons*? and she said Yes, I will give you that one. This choice was good on three levels because (1) she gave me that one, and (2) Milhouse really belongs in the not-hot dag category, but if she was going to be such an American imperialist with her no-*Neighbours* rule then I wasn't going to let on about Milhouse. Annabel knows *The Simpsons* is Dad's and my favorite show but I know she doesn't know who Milhouse is, so really it was (3) me giving her that one, but on the sly.

Anyway.

It would be easy to place too many cute guys into the hot dag category, so we noted some important exceptions taken directly from Annabel's imaginary love life. Someone who's hot but not a dag would be Leonardo's character in *Titanic*, which is Annabel's favorite movie of all time but one which I personally think was pretty stupid and cheesy. Leonardo's character is too handsome and confident. Annabel's heart will still go on for him forever and ever, but dag? No way. Annabel's crush-love, Ben? He's a spunk who's both popular and handsome, and knows it. So not a dag.

Moving on to the category of not-so-hot dags but we still heart them, a famous ancient TV example would be Screech from *Saved by the Bell*. Our friend Maurice, the pink-robed crazy man, probably qualifies as a not-hot dag, except Annabel added that Maurice is really only famous in Australia right now so he doesn't count, and it's only because Maurice seemed to be a sore subject for her that I didn't argue her anti-Aussie conceit. Annabel nominated as a not-hot dag some American phenom called Clay Aiken, but Annabel put in the disclaimer that no one will even remember who he is in ten years so maybe he was a bad example, to which I answered, Who is Clay Aiken, anyway? In this category of dagginess, I pointed out a great home-grown Australian example in Slim Dusty, an ancient, cowboy country singer that Mum and Dad love listening to. He sang great, twangy drinking tunes but was not a heartthrob AT ALL. However, Annabel said that guy is dead and we're trying to disqualify the dead dags on the basis of there being too many of them; she only made the one exception for President Truman because she said I should know how dagginess relates to American history now that I live here. Then she added that people will remember Clay Aiken way longer than Slim Dusty, which I said as a belief system is totally wrong and yet another huge example of American arrogance so get over it, Annabel.

Finally, we agreed on the nomination of Annabel's stepbro Wheaties as the ultimate dag. He's the boy who's like a walking encyclopedia of facts and figures, whether it's *Billboard* charts' number ones since 1957, or baseball statistics since the time when baseball was a stickball game on the street. Annabel noted that Wheaties is a fanatic baseball supporter and he really only compiles facts for American League teams, but he's not a maven when it comes to National League teams, which according to Annabel is like a Coke versus Pepsi distinction. I wanted to know what's a "maven," and Annabel said she doesn't know but according to Bubbe, Wheaties is one.

Although Wheaties is from New York, he's a big rebel (ace dag quality, btw) in that he supports the Boston Red Sox and never, ever, the loathsome Yankees. I actually understood this part of Annabel's rant because our Dad is a Mets supporter and even though I'm Australian, I know all about the Bronx Bombers and how they're this team that money bought but who have no heart or substance. Oh, our dad Jack: DAG DAG DAG! But he's a dad, so he's neither the hot kind nor the not-so-hot kind, he's just the dad-dag kind.

But back to our dag superhero, Wheaties. He's always the shortest person in his class, and he's too skinny because, we suspect, he spends too much time computing and not enough time eating, even though the great and powerful Bubbe is always trying to tempt him with a good brisket and egg-cream soda (ewww!). He has strawberry blond hair, leaning more on the strawberry side, and blond eyelashes, leaning more on the albino side, but he has what Bubbe calls "such a nice face" that you can't not look at him and not think, *awwww*. You just can't say that in front of him, or he will turn not-daggy and all-out hostile.

At his bar mitzvah party, Wheaties had a karaoke machine with video monitors set up, and he sang pop tunes followed by heavy-metal thrasher anthems followed by rap songs—VERSATILE! His party coincided with the one time I got to visit New York City, and I can vouch for the fact that all the shy girls who were sitting quietly at their tables realized Wheaties' dag potential within two karaoke songs. You could tell those girls wanted to dance but they were too embarrassed to ask any boy, or too embarrassed about not being asked by any boy, but within minutes of Wheaties hitting the mike, they were screaming at him like he was a rock star and dancing all over the place.

Maybe what makes a dag fall into the hot variety comes down to simple confidence. It's like the great line in the sand separating the haves from the have-nots.

Right now, Wheaties falls somewhere in the middle of the hot/not-so-hot dag range. Annabel and I awarded Wheaties the Dag with the Most Potential to Cross Over to the Hot Category prize. Sure, he's a bony little guy at age fourteen, but we have big belief in his makeover ability as he gets older, and we suspect he's the nerd that will win the hot girl in the end—or at least by senior prom, so he has a few years to work on his transformation. Annabel said we're bullish on his prospects, and I said that sounds gross but she assured me it's not. She said it means that if Wheaties was a stock on the New York Stock Exchange and we were investors, we would BUY BUY BUY.

In conclusion, we decided we will approve of the lucky girl Wheaties wins so long as she's nice and dresses well (that's Annabel's concern, not mine, for the record) and so long as she appreciates Wheaties for being the ultimate dag he is.

End of hike, end of report, time for brekkie!

Chapter 5

WHEATIES

If I were the director, writer, and star of *Wheaties: The Movie*—the good, character-driven, thought-provoking kind of film, but with at least a few quality car chases and some token beautiful women wearing bikinis, but that doesn't make me a sexist for wanting that, it is *my* movie—here's how I would imagine my opening scene. The camera follows me strutting through the airport, the short guy with all the cool. The audience may assume, because of my yellow alligator shirt with the upturned collar, the red corduroy pants hemmed too long, and my tight weave of short strawberry hair that adores any form of gel hair product for men, that they're in for some updated version of *Revenge of the Nerds*, but little things will clue them in otherwise. There's the latest technological device I've invented myself, clutched in my hand like a Bible. An airport worker walks by, then realizes it's me, the famous Wheaties guy, and the airport worker doubles back to high-five me, saying, "Little Al with the big cool! I can't believe it's you!" My cover now blown by his loud pronouncement, I am soon swarmed by college-girl groupies wanting to feed off me like mosquitoes.

Theme song music is both key and should be derivative, so my opening-scene movie strut will borrow the theme from the movie *Shaft*. As some soul-singing dude with a deep voice asks something about, Who's the cat that won't cop out when there's danger all about?, instead of answering, "Shaft, right on!" the back-up singers will shout out, "Al, Big Al, yeah!" My fan base may be young, but don't worry that they won't appreciate my new version of an old theme song. They've all been to my Web site and heard the audio sample from the original. They know the *Shaft* song comes from a personal '70s-movie-classic favorite of mine, and they've downloaded the theme song eons ago. The fans get it because that's just how it works with me. Either you get me or you don't.

In real life, the person who gets me—Tia—picked me up at LAX, and not the person who doesn't—my mom. I like Tia because she is like my other step-mom, Angelina. They both have long, pretty hair that smells really good, the key difference being that Tia has long, silky black hair that she usually wears in a braid hanging down her back instead of bothering with the shampoo-commercial glamour brunette thing like Angelina does.

On the ride home from LAX, traffic hardly moved along the freeway because of construction, but the car's near idleness and the sounds of honking and jackhammering did not irritate Tia. When Dad drives in backed-up traffic in Manhattan, he slams his car horn every two seconds and flails his arms in the air, like he's shocked traffic could be that bad, even though it always is. Tia, she sits in the driver seat, sometimes humming a little, sometimes with a little smile at the corners of her mouth, as if she's got lots of pleasant things to think about instead of the maddening traffic right outside her windshield.

Tia's a much better driver than Dad—and especially better than Mom. When Mom drives, she's impatient like Dad, then add in a cell-phone headset she's shouting into, plus the In-N-Out burger she's chomping on because the only time she has to eat is in the car. Then Mom acts all surprised when other drivers stick their hands out their car windows to make rude gestures at her.

Tia didn't learn to drive until she was thirty years old and had moved to Los Angeles from New York, but driving with her is safe and smooth, like she's a professional driver who's been doing it all her life. Another key difference between my stepmom types is that Tia's much quieter than Angelina, so after ten long minutes of smooth driving, with no talking between us, and the

Spanish-language radio station playing songs I didn't understand because I take French at school, *merci*, I had to kick-start some conversation. Since I'm polite, I waited until after a song ended and Tia had stopped singing along to the radio before coming out with the question I'd been dying to ask since the moment my plane landed. "Tia, did Angelina call and say anything about Annabel coming over?"

See how I asked about Annabel and not Lucy? I'm clever that way. I said Annabel's name because I knew her name alone implied that where Annabel went, so went Lucy. They're like two halves of a whole that way. I didn't include Lucy's name because Tia is very smart, and I knew if I so much as said Lucy's name aloud, Tia might instantly suspect that I am crazy in love with Lucy. We're not talking crush here. We're talking ready-to-propose-as-soon-as-she-even-notices-I-exist love. Lucy's not even Jewish—that's how much I adore her.

Tia reached over and gave my arm a little stroke. I think all girls should be more like Tia. She seems very content with who she is and always makes other people around her feel more comfortable. Her face is never hidden under makeup, and she dresses very casually in old blue jeans and T-shirts. She's not caught up trying to appear sophisticated like every teenage girl I know. If all girls were more like Tia, it wouldn't take so long for boys to relax around them. If Lucy could be less mysterious and more transparent like Tia, I wouldn't have to all the time wonder—does Lucy like me, like, like-like me, or does she think of me as just a friend, or hold on, does she even think about me at all the way that I think about her: 24/7/365?

Tia answered, "Yeah, Al. Angelina called, and we made plans to meet them over at Venice Beach a couple days from now, after you get settled in." Tia's such a quiet person that sometimes when I hear her voice, I'm surprised by it all over again. Tia's voice is all Bronx by way of the Dominican Republic, with quick words in a hard-edged, thick NY accent that you almost need a decoder to decipher. Her accent is not at all what you would expect from someone with such a mellow, relaxed air about her. "We have plenty of time to hang out with Angelina and that whole crew since your mommy will be working very late at the office tonight. She felt bad about missing your first day here, but I told her just stay at the office until her deal closes, and then she can spend quality time with us instead of sporadic time interrupted by calls from the office. Right? It's better to have time with Mommy when you can really see her; so you and me, we'll have adventures on our own today."

"Mommy" is what Tia calls her own mom back in the Bronx. Tia talks to her mother on the phone in Spanish every morning, getting updates on nieces and nephews and cousins back home, and also hearing about Tia's mommy's crazy boss at the law firm who throws things at his office walls until Tia's mommy sets the *loco* man straight even though she's just his secretary and he's the boss.

"Mommy" is not what I would call my mother. If I have to address her, I go with "Mom," but mostly I avoid addressing her directly. I'm not "Al" or "Wheaties" to her. In fact, Mom's pretty much the only person who calls me by my given name, Alan. *How's school going, Alan?* or *Still getting the top grades, Alan, so you can go to Columbia, like Dad and me?* Mom's a top partner at a big law firm here in Los Angeles who brags about the fact that she bills *over three thousand hours a year, Alan!* Compute the math on those billable hours versus the total hours in a year and then it makes sense why I prefer to live with Dad in New York than with Mom in LA. Dad works a lot too, but he's practically a slacker compared to Mom.

I don't dread visiting with Mom so much now that Tia lives with her. Tia used to be a paralegal at Mom's law firm back when Mom still lived in New York. Like Tia's mommy, Tia never hesitated to tell off Mom when Mom got so stressed at the office that she took it out on everyone else. The difference between Tia and Tia's mommy would be that Tia's mother has been married for years to Tia's dad who's a mellow guy like Tia and nothing at all like the crazy boss, while Tia and her crazy boss, who happened to be my mom, decided maybe they had feelings for each other that weren't professional. Since Tia and Mom kinda sorta loved each other, they figured they shouldn't work together anymore, but should live together instead. That's how Tia and Mom came to move to LA, because they wanted to start fresh; so now Mom works for a different law firm out here, and Tia works part-time at a volunteer legal-aid job, which leaves the rest of her time free to make great food and to hang out with me when I visit. She also happens to make Mom a much happier, nicer person. That is, when Mom bothers to even be around.

I've never known my mom well enough to truly miss her the way, say, Annabel has missed her father since he left New York to start a new family. I feel like I love my mother like I'm supposed to, but in a remote way, like she gave birth to me and I appreciate that, but I've never really known her, or she me. So logically speaking, how could anyone expect us to be any mother-son dream team of tender emotions and cards and flowers on Mother's Day?

In the movie of my life there will probably be a climactic scene where I have an epic breakdown and admit that sometimes I worry whether I am a bad person and a bad son for not really missing Mom. I was in kindergarten when she and Dad divorced, and since then, I see her for about a total of only six weeks out of the year, during school breaks. What's to miss? When it comes time for my big movie scene, the camera will probably go in for a close-up shot as I throw my arms in the air and wail, *Will God punish me for being a bad son and not loving his mother enough?* And

God, who has an interest in me personally due to my 95th percentile PSAT scores before I've even officially entered high school, answers back with a thunderous roar: *She who giveth you life, and you, Wheaties of the Upper West Side, who taketh that gift for granted and besmirch thine own mother! You shalt be strucketh down, right in front of Fairway at peak shopping hours during the time of Sukkot! Learn to honor thy mother properly or watcheth thy back at Broadway and Seventy-fourth!*

The audience will be shocked by this big reveal of vulnerability both from God and from that unlikely antihero of cool, Wheaties aka Al aka Alan, or, as seen through the camera lens, the blubbering idiot in the movie of his life. Many Oscar nominations will surely follow, although the big award will go to whatever old timer deserved to win twenty years ago and the Academy is feeling guilty about so they give him mine. Adding insult to injury and possible eternal damnation for the Academy voters, the hot young actor with the lisp wins the supporting-actor nod over God. See, God only got nominated for the supporting role on account of his omniscience and not for the few but crucial lines in the climactic scene of my movie, whereas the lisp guy has a genuine disability and therefore had to overcome more adversity to achieve his cinematic brilliance.

"Do you have a hat with you?" Tia asked. "You have to be the palest *chico* I've ever seen, so we're gonna have to pick up a hat and some sunscreen before taking you to Venice Beach. I don't want you to get all sunburned like last time and then have your dad call and ream your mommy out after you get home."

"I have a hat!" I said. I reached to the car floor for my Teenage Mutant Ninja Turtles backpack that I've had since kindergarten and still carry solely for the benefit of Annabel's horror. I took out the hat from the backpack to show Tia.

Tia laughed. "I'm gonna let the backpack slide, but you call that a hat? If you wear that to the beach, I just cannot be responsible for the looks you get—you're asking for it. But hey, that's what I respect about you, Al. Wearing a bright yellow girl's hat in public doesn't faze you one bit. You're your own man, always have been." Like I said, Tia gets me.

I placed the hat on my head and admired myself in the sun visor mirror. The floppy yellow hat, wide-brimmed with flaps falling over the ears, did look funny against my white skin and light eyebrows, but the effect was worth it just to calculate how many seconds it will take Annabel seeing me in this hat before she hits the mall to find me a new one. That will leave Lucy free to hang out with me, just me! *Mwah-ha-ha.* The hat belongs to Lucy, anyway. She left it at our apartment last year when she visited from Australia, and I've been holding on to it since, waiting for my opportunity to return it to her in person.

I'm not shallow. I love Lucy for more than just how pretty she is. I love her Australian accent, which sounded so nice when Annabel and I tried to teach her New York style curse-outs. She could make the most vulgar words sound like poetry. She's different from other girls too. She's not obsessed with wearing the right labels or being popular. Lucy always gave up her seat on the subway to pregnant ladies or old people before anyone else noticed those folks needed seats. Lucy loved to hold Ariel, who had just been born when Lucy visited us in NYC, and read stories to Ariel at night, even though Ariel was so small and swaddled she couldn't have had any idea what Lucy was saying. And unlike her stepsister, Annabel, Lucy never tried to give me a makeover. She just said, *Plaid pants with a frilly pirate top, yeah? Hey Wheaties, if that's what works for you.* I suspect Lucy might be like Tia: she gets me.

In the torture scene of my movie, I will probably admit that Annabel also gets me and appreciates me, but she's related now and therefore almost contractually bound to defend me. I am on record for gratitude to Annabel for saving my tush many times last year at school when kids decided to make Wheaties their token joke for the day—that is, on the days they didn't want help with their math homework. Two things kids at our school learned not to joke about with Annabel were her clothes or her stepbrother Wheaties, because that girl can slap down if you get her started, so don't get on her bad side. But I'm a year past bar mitzvah, manhood age now, and I am not going to worry that

Annabel won't have my back next year when we start different high schools. I'll be fine on my own because of the luuuvvv I'll be getting from my future, passionate, long-distance relationship with Lucy, who will fall in love with me this summer. I'll start off freshman year of high school by hanging pictures in my locker of Lucy in her surfer wet suit, or Lucy in the blue dress designed by Annabel, and make all the high school dude-men drool with envy over scrawny little Wheaties with the Aussie babe girlfriend. Yeah, that'll work out good.

I wonder if in the year since I've seen Lucy, if she's figured out that her attending my bar mitzvah was better to me than the piles of presents, moolah, and supposed official entry into manhood that I received on my big day. Does she replay the night over and over in her head like I do? Has she come to suspect that when I went prehistoric with the karaoke machine selections and sang "2 Become 1" by the Spice Girls, I was really singing the song for her and not for the group of girls that had surprisingly crowded around the stage after I got the show rolling with "Get the Party Started"?

With Lucy's hat on my head, I made some sexy James Bond faces in the car mirror, trying out a *Oh, you were saying something to me, darling?* look followed by the vintage *Gorgeous, I can think of nothing I'd love better from you than a . . .* look, when Tia announced, "Here we are, home! Westwood, the Manhattan of

LA." Then at the same time, Tia and I both shouted, "NOT!" which is our favorite private joke. Tia and I suspect maybe it's all the beautiful weather in LA draining people's intelligence that makes them call Westwood the Manhattan of LA, because that assessment is plain wrong.

Mom and Tia live on the top floor of a big high-rise building in Westwood, an area in the western part of the city where the UCLA campus is. The main drag of Westwood is like driving through a cement canyon, because Westwood has lots of business and residential high-rise buildings. But just because an area has tall buildings doesn't give it character like New York. You can't walk out of a penthouse apartment building in Westwood and get a great bagel or hail a simple taxi, for example. The sidewalk in Westwood is clean and new, and empty when it's not business hours. When you go outside in New York, you're likely to bounce around the pavement, dodging lots of people and dog poo— or rats rummaging through the garbage on the street; ideally the rat situation happens when Annabel is with you because who doesn't love hearing Annabel's signature ear-piercing scream, the one so hysterical she probably wakes up the mummies at the Metropolitan Museum on the other side of Central Park?

What Mom and Tia's apartment in Westwood has over New York is the view from the top. Their apartment has huge glass windows you can look out to see vistas like in a painting: palm tree-lined avenues, snow-covered mountains, or the sun setting over the mighty Pacific at dusk, with the smog turning the sunset into this psychedelic pink-gray toxic glow that's more awesome than scary. Really.

Mom must be into amazing window views, because she has a corner office at the top of her skyscraper office building in downtown LA. From her office in the sky, you can see the whole LA basin, including the "HOLLYWOOD" sign, all the way to Westwood, and up to Malibu, depending on the smog. Actually, being surrounded by huge glass windows with incredible views is how I think of Mom, when I do think of her: at the top of the world, in a fishbowl.

Chapter 6

Annabel

Lucy is a beach snob and I am a clothes snob, but Venice Beach meets both our high standards. Lucy is psyched on the Venice Beach scene because it's stocked with her kind of people—bodyboarding, surfing, volleyball-playing, sun-worshipping sporty folk like her. Venice Beach is Lucy's American version of Sydney's Bondi Beach. For me, the scene also reminds me of another place—Manhattan—and that's because being a New Yorker, I can truly appreciate the quality freak show found here at Venice Beach.

I'm not a person who likes to sit still, but under my very big hat, sunglasses, and SPF-40 sunscreen, the general suckiness that is LA in comparison to NY hasn't been all torture. I've been totally content to pass the afternoon sitting on a boardwalk bench, sketching the mixture of surf and urban chic worn on all the freakish hard bodies here. With bodies like that, this girl here is certainly not going to wear her swimsuit on the beach! Since I'm not a flasher like the people here seem to be, for my fashion statement today, I've gone with capri pants and a three-quarters sleeve, light cotton blouse to minimize skin exposure.

Even if I don't approve of their fashion choices (or lack of them), these Venice Beach bikini bodies do make for excellent artistic study. I've just now finished a cartoon sketch of the girl volleyball players on the beach who are dressed like they're trying out for the kind of naughty club where girls dance on poles. The girl volleyball players trounced the opposing team of college frat boys, as the guys had a hard time paying attention to the volleyball what with all the jiggling going on from the girl side of the net. The bubble caption over the boys' heads: *Dude, do you think those are real?*

That's just the beach—there's plenty more entertainment to see and hear on the boardwalk at Venice Beach. In New York, the best amateur entertainment is underground, in the subway stations, where the air most definitely is not as fresh and breezy as the ocean air here. Even so, I kinda miss the guitar-playing bluesman at the Museum of Natural History subway stop in Manhattan. He's as good as the saxophone-playing guy I heard once on the train going to Bloomie's was atrocious. The sax guy's instrument looked like it had been plucked from the Dumpster, and the sound it made was so bad that it was obvious the guy didn't know how to play a note—he just puffed into the mouthpiece, and the tinny, off-key sounds the sax made caused the train passengers to cringe and moan in despair. The sax guy was considerate, however—he would let subway riders pay him *not* to play. But the Venice Beach street performers might have it all over NYC for craziness. Maybe it's something about the gorgeous sunshine, palm trees, and ocean breeze that attracts such a high volume of freak performers here. In one afternoon, I've seen some great break dancing complete with Olympic-worthy acrobatics, some pop star wannabes who put even the worst *American Idol* rejects to shame, and a lady opera singer who somehow managed to put a hip-hop beat into the death scene aria from Bubbe's favorite opera, *La Traviata*.

Even Bebe, sitting alongside me on the boardwalk, dribbling an ice cream down her shirt because she's two and doesn't care about messing up the OshKosh overalls outfit personally assembled by her big sister Annabel, stood up on our bench to dance to the hip-hopera lady. Now that I've been here for almost two weeks, Bebe is getting used to me again and will let me stay with her without Penny being present—although the ice cream bribery does help. And I have gotten used to calling her Bebe, which does fit her better as a name, I think. Beatrice always sounded like an old person's name to me.

I still wish I was in Sydney for summer vacation, but this LA thing is working out okay so far.

LA has some obsession with perfection: perfect bodies, perfect weather, perfect cars. Today, Annabel the Moody, as Lucy thinks I don't know she calls me, is perfectly content here. It's a perfect summer day (of course) and everyone is enjoying themselves, and I can't help but feel a little proud that I am the person who connects us all. If you drew our family map, I'd be the center circle that everyone else goes through, like I'm the Times Square subway station connecting all the subway lines to one another. If it weren't for me, Angelina wouldn't be a "shark biscuit"—someone new to surfing in Aussiespeak—in the ocean right now with her surfing instructor, Lucy. Baby Ariel goes through the Annabel center circle, straight into the arms of her new auntie, Tia, who's got her in the snuggly taking a nap while Tia reads a book on the beach and whisper-sings Spanglish lullabies in Ariel's ear like she's one of Tia's nieces back home. Last stop on the Annabel Transit Authority connector link would be Wheaties the NY Mensch, who I can see walking toward me on the boardwalk, alongside Lady Penny and Sir Angus of Oz, all three of them slurping smoothies.

Of course, if we charted a map of just the important people—the high school-age ones, fuhgedabout the parental types—it would start with me and Lucy, the core set of steps. But now that we've got Wheaties here in LA with us, and Ben almost here, we can expand the map, because now we're two steps forward to being a core four. Not a bad map for a girl who never wanted or expected to be anything other than an only child, a lonely dot in the middle of a small boring map.

I had coached Bebe on what to say to Wheaties when he, Penny, and Angus met back up with us on the boardwalk bench where I was waiting for them, like I'm Grand Central Station. "Here, Wheaties," Bebe said in her half-American, half-Aussie accent, handing him a new Kangol hat made sticky by the vanilla ice cream goo on her little hand, "we bought you a new hat. Now take off Lucy's!"

Now that Wheaties is in LA, the city feels right. Even if he's not staying with us, I've gotten so used to having him around that I strangely miss him when he's gone. We did, after all, spend the better part of our last school year bonded in Bubbe's den doing homework together, refugees from Harvey and Angelina and their alternating fights/long meaningful silences back at our apartment a few blocks away.

"Hey, nerd," I said to Wheaties.

"Hey, fashion disaster," he said to me.

Ah, just like old times.

Penny looked confused. She doesn't get New York insult/affection. She took Bebe in her arms and sat down on the bench next to me with Bebe on her lap. "Did I miss something?" she asked. Hmm. Bubbe➡ Bebe. Bebe➡Bubbe. My grandma on my mom's side and my sister on my dad's side aren't connected at all, but their names almost are.

"No worries," I assured Penny, using the Aussie expression for "everything's cool." Folks from Down Under use that expression almost as often as they say "great!" but pronounced "graayate."

Penny glanced at her watch. "The rest of the gang should be meeting us back at this spot in about fifteen minutes. It's been nice to have a day at the beach, hey? I didn't think I could like the beach here, but Venice Beach, it's *fair dinkum*."

"Fair dinkum?" Wheaties asked.

"It's Aussie for 'real, genuine,'" I said. If I ever decide to toss my fashion-design career ambitions, I'll probably be qualified as a UN translator by the time this summer is over. It's important to keep your options open, according to Bubbe.

Penny said, "I've enjoyed this day so much, you know what I'm going to do? Drive home myself! That's right, me, in the driver side, on the freeway, at rush hour. Fearless! Queen of the World!" In tribute to me and my favorite movie, my stepmom threw her arms in the air like she was Leonardo at the bow of the doomed ship. Then Penny's arms dropped and she paused for a moment, perhaps realizing the complicated logistics that seem to go along with getting around in LA: several people, more than one car. Penny added, "But Angelina rides in my car, not Tia's. Angelina drove my car here today, but if I'm going to get us back home, I need her in the passenger side."

I have to give Angelina credit. I don't know many women that would make friends with her ex's new wife like Angelina has with Penny since we've arrived in LA. I don't think it's because they both have older and younger daughters who are the same age. Jack and Angelina might pretend to like each other for my sake, but Angelina and Penny seem to genuinely like each other, and for more than the convenience of one mom who can take the other's baby to the playground along with her own to give the other mom some free time.

Penny is freaking terrified of driving here in LA— something about her not being able to adjust to driving on the right instead of the left side, combined with all the traffic, and the noise of kids in the car distracting her. Penny could tackle all the responsibilities of raising two children on her own in Melbourne after her first husband's sudden death, yet she's afraid to get behind the simple American car wheel. Angelina says Penny will never adapt and be able to thrive here like the rest of her family if Penny is trapped in her house by this fear, so Angelina has taken it upon herself to be Penny's driving teacher. It's rather like the blind leading the blind. Angelina has lived in Manhattan almost her whole life and knows more about hailing a taxi than driving a car, but somehow, because she drove cross country once when she came home from college, and because she rents cars whenever she travels to other cities, Angelina thinks she's qualified as a driving expert.

"What's for dinner?" Wheaties asked. For his first night in LA with us, we're having a BBQ in the backyard at Jack and Penny's. Maybe my family is crazy and all over the map, but I think it's nice that we can come from so many different directions and still make it all work. We're in LA and working on being perfect, after all. My dread may be melting with all this sunshine, warmth, and morning hikes with Lucy, but the Bubbe in me whispers, *How long can the good times last before everyone is fighting again like a family is supposed to do?*

For now, the person I have to thank most for all the good feeling is my stepmom, Penny. She's the one who decided we should have a family BBQ tonight, and she's the one who, I don't know why and I don't really want to know how, has made it all right between Jack and Angelina so we can all hang together and it's not awkward. She's the one who suggested we include Tia and Wheaties in our day adventure. Maybe Penny can be so generous because she's the one who scored the happy marriage, the one still so blissfully in love with my dad that she's willing to take on all the complications he brought with him. I wish my mom had that—a relationship where two people grow stronger together despite their obstacles, instead of hurting each other. I used to wish Angelina had with Jack what Jack has with Penny, but Jack and Angelina have been apart long enough now, I almost don't remember what it was like when I was little and lived with my real parents. What seemed so natural then, seems laughable to imagine now—me, Jack, Angelina, one family unit on our own, with no Penny, Lucy, and Angus, no Bebe and Ariel, no Wheaties and Tia, and one little Manhattan apartment instead of us spread across the globe.

I said, "Wheaties, in your honor, it's koala tails on the barbie for dinner tonight."

"Really?" Angus the seven-year-old vegetarian said with a horrified face.

"No, not really, Angus," Penny said. She passed Bebe to my lap and picked up Angus for a cuddle. "Annabel is engaging in what's called sarcasm. You know, the trait she's passed on so successfully to Lucy?" Penny winked at me. Angus stuck his purple smoothie tongue out at me.

Wheaties said, "How about BEN burgers for dinner?"

My heart flipped over hearing that word. I must have gone into a trance state, because I didn't realize I'd made a sound in response until Wheaties muttered, "Do you realize you do that? You scream at just the mention of the name Ben? And sometimes Lucy does it too, to go along with you, and I don't think you should encourage her like that because at least Lucy usually has more common sense than to do that shrieking girl thing." Wheaties tried to sound all casual and hide his jealousy, but that was hard to do on a face as pale as his. The white skin on his face splotched with red, revealing his mad love for Lucy, like a glaring blood stain at a crime scene.

"Ben!" Angus said, excited, getting over the koala-burger suggestion in a New York minute. "Ben arrives tomorrow, right, Mum?"

Ben's like the axis that we mere mortals should revolve around. The long-distance gap on the map between Ben and his former steps and me, the future love of his life, is finally ready to close!

Finally, something "graayate" that could turn this LA summer into what else: perfection!

Chapter 7

Lucy

Aside from the beautiful weather and the random celebrity sightings (I'm sure it was Tori Spelling's BMW that Mum cut off on the 405 freeway on our way back from Venice Beach!), what I like most about our new life in LA is the pool in our backyard. Dad almost didn't buy this house because of the pool and the cost to maintain it, but the pool made Mum happy so that made the house all right by Dad.

At first I didn't like the pool because it gave Mum an excuse to stay home and not drive. Dad sold reluctant Mum on the idea of us moving from Australia to LA by pointing out that she wouldn't have to work at a job she didn't like any longer, that she could be a full-time mum and work on her photography now that his career was doing so well. What that's meant, however, is Mum wanting to take endless pictures of me,

Angus, and Bebe playing in the pool, making the pool sometimes feel more like a jail sentence than a privilege. Um, could we *go* somewhere, please?

Also, when we first got here, Angus loved the pool so much he decided to liberate his goldfish into it when none of us were looking. It took Josephine Snickercross to explain to Angus what means "chlorine" and "ritual sacrifice," and Dad going back to the pet shop for replacement goldfish, before Angus would step back into the pool after that particular disaster. He's still a little wary of it. He'll come in, but only when Dad is around.

Now Mum's driving (thanks heaps, Angelina!), and our pool and backyard have become hangout central since all the *A* girls have decamped to LA for the summer. The pool isn't big enough for proper laps Aussie Speedo style, but it was big enough for Angelina and me to float on hot pink inflated lounge chairs while we sipped Kool-Aids with straws, holding our cups from the inflated drink holder in one hand and crinkled wet script pages in the other, as we rehearsed lines for Angelina's callback audition the next day. We went for the full movie-star-by-the-pool LA effect, wearing wide-brimmed hats and rhinestone-specked cat-eye sunglasses along with our bathing suits.

ANGELINA (as the sexy defendant on trial for really bad illegal stuff):
How do I plead? I plead guilty to being in

love with the wrong man, a man who led me
down the righteously wrong path and used me
for his own criminal gain. But I plead, most
emphatically (Angelina lets out a drama-
queen gasp and then whips off her sunglasses
with A+ exaggerated effort) NOT GUILTY to
setting that man up for murder!

**LUCY (as the smoldering prosecution
attorney man determined to bring the
defendant down, despite being madly
in love with her):**
Objection, Your Honor! Defendant is leading
the jury with histrionics and . . .

**WHEATIES (as the fed-up chick judge),
sitting at the edge of the pool, dangling
his feet in the water:**
OVERRULED!

Our brill performances received thunderous
applause from the patio-deck-tier audience: Mum,
Tia, Annabel, and Maurice, sitting under the circu-
lar patio umbrella table, munching nachos. The
babies weren't around to cheer our exceptional performances—and my properly pronouncing the
word "histrionics" after only ten tries—because the
day in the sun had spent them. They had zonked
out in Bebe's crib as soon as we got home from the
beach. Dad and Angus were hidden inside the

house working on Angus's aquarium.

Let's count: Angelina has been here two weeks, and of all the eight evenings she, Annabel, and Ariel have spent here having dinner with us, Dad has spent six of those dinners dividing his time between eating at the table and taking calls in his office or hiding out with Angus. The other two nights Dad stayed late at the studio with Maurice.

Dad doesn't need to hide, really. The atmosphere in the backyard is mellower than he could imagine. I happen to know Angelina taught Mum a trick Angelina learned from being a summer-camp counselor years ago, which is that Kool-Aid spiked with the little bottles that adults buy on airplanes makes for some good times. Angelina and Mum have developed their own tag-team rhythm of tending to needy babies, grocery shopping, practice driving, and hanging out by the pool with their Kool-Aids once the younger ones are in bed. I don't imagine Mum ever reckoned her first real friend in LA would be her husband's ex, but then again, Mum once told me she never thought she'd travel beyond the little dot at the bottom of the world that is Melbourne, and now look at all the places she's been. And look at the person she's become. I think my mum is pretty cool.

When Angelina and Mum hang out at night, once the little ones are asleep, Annabel and I sit on the pool ledge, dangling our feet in the chilly nighttime water, talking and laughing, while Angelina and Mum do the same at the patio table. Sometimes Annabel and I just pretend to talk, but really we're watching the mums. My mum, who with her pale skin, short bob of black hair, and intense black eyes, is like the goth polar opposite of glamour girl Angelina, will place her hands on the patio table and say, "Madge, I don't know what to do with these brittle hands I get from dish washing." Angelina will do one of her vintage hair-flipping maneuvers and answer with the fake importance of some Harvard talking-head genius, "Have you tried Fresh4U dish-washing liquid? Feel your freshest self!" Then Mum and Angelina break out in hysterics like they invented comedy or something, and Annabel and I roll our eyes at their Kool-Aid cocktail not-funny funniness. Mum and Angelina's scenes often coincide with the exact moment Dad has gotten up the courage to approach, because he sees them laughing together and turns back around from the sliding door, gesturing quietly to Annabel to follow him into his home office so they can have their alone time.

This late evening, with Angelina's audition rehearsal complete, Angelina took the crinkled pages from my hand and passed them off to Mum, who clipped the pages onto the clothesline to dry. Annabel waded into the pool to join us. Annabel will wear a swimsuit only at our house, around people who know her. She's very weird about her body. She'll wear the shortest of skirts but she won't wear a swimsuit when we're at the beach. She looks beautiful no matter what she wears, so I don't understand the problem.

I told her, "I love your new swimsuit! You should have worn that at the beach today." She was wearing a gray tankini that covered up just about every part of her torso except her belly button.

Annabel waded into the water, then held her nose between her fingers and dropped to the floor of the pool. She emerged back up with a big splash and then took her long hair between her hands to squeeze out the excess water. "Thank you," Annabel said. "Gray is the new black."

I tossed my sunglasses and hat to the side of the pool and took a dive down under. I swam over to where Wheaties' feet dangled in the water. With Annabel in the pool, we had enough people for a water-volleyball game if we set up the net. I tugged on Wheaties' feet from under the water and he kicked back. When I came up for air, I said, "Why don't you come all the way in?"

Angelina answered for him like she was his real mum. "He had pneumonia when he was a child and still catches cold easily. The doctor doesn't recommend him swimming unless it's a heated pool." Angelina lifted the inflated ball floating in the pool and threw it to Wheaties.

Wheaties missed the ball with dag-worthy lack of effort. He pointed to his stepmom. "What she said," he confirmed.

I had to cross my arms over my chest as I stood in the water before him, because Wheaties doesn't seem to know how to zone his eyes in on mine when talking to me. His eyes always wander down, like he has no control over them. I'm almost ready to formally introduce Wheaties' eyes to my boozies.

Lucy's boozies:
Why, hello Wheaties. We're Lucy's boozies.
Stop staring at us or we'll be forced to get
a restraining order.

Wheaties' eyes:
Did you say something? We couldn't
concentrate because we're too busy staring
at . . . well, you know.

Maurice waved a script from the patio table. "Oh Angelina darling," he called over to us. "Uncle Maurice needs your help running lines for tomorrow, hey?" Maurice may as well move in with us at this point. He was over here a lot before the A girls arrived, but now that he's discovered Angelina, we can't get rid of him. He says Angelina is a "muse," and he can't rehearse his script unless she is there to read the other parts with him. Dad wants Maurice's rehearsals to go as smoothly as possible, so he goes along with Maurice, even if it means having Angelina over at the house more than he might like. I suspect Maurice is just too lazy and insecure to get a real girlfriend, and Angelina makes a nice-looking substitute, and one who can do funny character voices for his scripts. Annabel just ignores him, like he doesn't exist. She's good at that.

Dad came out of the sliding door of the house as Angelina stepped out of the pool. He stood by her while she toweled off and asked her in a low voice, "Can you be sure to read with Maurice until he knows his lines backward and forward? His show has only got a midseason pickup, and if he blows any more takes tomorrow, the network will cancel the show before it even gets an airing."

Angelina answered, "I'll be glad to help. Just remember that help when the bill comes for your portion of Annabel's school tuition."

Annabel was dipping her head under the water again and couldn't hear him, so Dad snapped at Angelina, "Oh, right! The school I never approved her even applying to, much less being enrolled at for four years."

Angelina wrapped the towel around herself and put her hand up in the "STOP" sign. "Don't even talk to the hand because the hand is bored already of this rant. She's going to that school in the fall whether you like it or not! I went there and I turned out just fine." Angelina knocked her head about for a moment to relieve her ears of pool water, so I'm not sure she heard Dad's sarcastic snort.

Dad took off his T-shirt and plunged into the water wearing his boxer shorts. "Hey Wheaties," he said.

"Throw the ball back in here!" Wheaties retrieved the ball and threw it back into the water. He couldn't return to the pool, however, as Angus had followed Dad from the house and had laid out *Aquarium Fishes of the World* on the patio deck for Wheaties to inspect with him. Wheaties had already been instructed by Josephine Snickercross, under the disguise of Lucy and her boozies, that when Angus brings out The Book, he cannot be ignored.

Dad tapped the ball first to Annabel. He asked her, "I can't believe my baby girl is starting high school. What do you think about going to your mother's alma mater, anyway? You remember, the one you never bothered to ask your old man's opinion about before choosing to go there?" He splashed some water at her playfully, and I don't know if Annabel realized Dad had set her into position for his classic game. I call it the 'Fess Up to Dad game because what he does is get me and Angus to play a game like Go Fish or water volleyball when we're being all mopey. We'll be having so much fun that we don't realize we're having A Talk until it's over and we're like spilling our guts, confessing we miss our gran in Melbourne, and LA is cool and all, but we can go home and spend Christmas with her, yeah?

Annabel flicked the ball over to me. She said, "Well, it's an excellent school with a great success rate in sending its students to the best colleges."

"That's your Bubbe repeating the school brochure."

Dad looked my way and said to me, "Toss me that ball, Luce, before Dad makes Annabel pay the price and does . . ." He dove under the water, where he tickled Annabel's feet. She screamed with laughter as he came back up, took a deep breath, and finished off his sentence with, ". . . that." I tossed him the ball, which he threw back over to Annabel, asking her, "What do *you* think? *I* am concerned that you're going to an elitist institution that's more about clothes competition and lack of diversity than a quality education."

Annabel punched the ball up in the air a few times like she was an LA Laker. "Dad! It's an all-girls school where we have to wear uniforms, so it's really more about shoe competition than any real clothes competition. And the absence of boys is the only diversity problem there. The school is near the UN and has students from all over the world, so that's not the reason why it could possibly be horrible. Try, all my friends from eighth grade are going to other schools and I won't know anyone there. And Wheaties helped me calculate a rich-girl to regular-girl ratio of the student body, and the probability of the school being overrun by mean girls with charge cards and diet pill issues is statistically quite high. That's the reason not to like the school."

Dad laughed. "How encouraging."

Annabel tossed the ball my way, and I helped her case by pointing out, "It's a snob-girl school, right?" Annabel's not (quite) a snob-girl or a rich girl, but she might be a delusional one, because I think she categorizes herself as a regular girl in her statistical probability thingie. Um, what regular girl's mum appears on telly promising that you too can *feel your freshest self?*

Annabel laughed as Dad did an underwater handstand in front of her. When he came back up, she allowed, "Dad, the fashion thing alone may very well kill me, but it's kind of a good school, even if it's populated by snob-girls. Lots of smart women have graduated from there—and not just the actress types like Mom, but like graduates who went on to become physicists and diplomats and CEOs. And I plan to go to the best college and become a major fashion force in this world, you know, so maybe Bubbe has a point about getting the best education? Cuz I'm not gonna drop out of college like you and Mom did!" Annabel works half as hard as me to get grades twice as good as mine, and yet she doesn't want to be seen in public wearing a swimsuit! For a brain who doesn't know she's a brain, she's completely illogical. I threw the ball back at her, but she lobbed it off her head like a soccer player, saying, "But the no-boys thing! I don't know how I'm going to deal with that. That's just, like, horrible."

Dad splashed her again. "Aha! At last we come upon Annabel's real concern. You know, the boy-free-zone aspect of your future high school is the one aspect I most approve of—aside from what sounds like a decent academic education for my Who Knew She Was So Motivated Darling Daughter? But if Ben thinks he's going to mind the gap in my daughter's boy education this summer, he's got a big obstacle in the way of that. ME!" Dad tackled Annabel in the water like he wanted to shield her from the air, and when she came up for breaths, she was laughing and smiling like Dad was funnier than Maurice.

Annabel may be the brain, but I'm the one who lives with and sees our dad every day. By my calculations, Dad's conclusion from the 'Fess Up to Dad game was probably that this school he and Angelina have been arguing over might not be such a bad choice for Annabel after all. I was so happy for her about Ben's arrival here; it's given her something exciting to look forward to after all the business with Harvey and Angelina, the dread of the new school, and the uncertainty of getting uprooted to LA for the summer. But now I felt a little bad for her too, because when it comes to the part about him being an obstacle to Ben, I don't think Dad was kidding.

Chapter 8

WHEATIES

Ben! All they talk about is Ben! They haven't seen the
dude since before my baby sister Ariel was just a dot
on the sonogram picture of Angelina's pregnant belly,
and now Ariel is almost walking and gurgling,
"Mama!" It's been a LOOOOONG while. Is all the
time and distance what's allowed Ben to transform
from boy-crush to he-man myth in Annabel's and
Lucy's minds? Is it possible to compute the length of
time/distance to growth of worship/adoration as a
mathematical equation? Maybe: 1.5 years x 10K miles
divided by infinite squeal-worship potential of two
14-year-old girls whose boy fantasies are obviously not
being met by today's television programmers aiming for
the teen audience? Wheaties' estimation: It's TV's fault!
There's no quality hunky-stupid-fake-misunderstood
hot guy character on a teen soap taking over their lives

right now, so Annabel and Lucy have to channel all that energy into talking about Ben nonstop.

The most frustrating part is I don't think Lucy even cares about Ben that much, at least not in the squeal-worship way. She goes along with the Ben worship to go along with her other half, Annabel. Why can't Annabel worship *me* so I could get some of that sec-ondhand Lucy attention?

I hate this Ben guy, and I've never even met him. He's probably one of those fellows who says "aaiit" like he's a white rapper wannabe and wears baggy pants hanging down from his butt on purpose, and not because he's from the too-skinny-Wheaties species of male. It's not my fault I'm all skin and bones. It's Mom's. I have her bad genes to thank that I'm a total lightweight in stature but a heavyweight in IQ points. Here's the IQ points back, Mom. I'll gladly sacrifice the points for one single semester of not being the little guy that gets flicked on the head by Ben-breed jocks passing me in the halls, jocks who downgrade their pummels to mere flicks because, after all, the dudes do like to peek over at my pop quiz French conjugations, *oui*?

I've decided I would authorize the complete drainage of my brain power in exchange for one day of being noticed by Lucy as a crush-worthy stud who's more than a "dag." If I hear that Aussie word come out of Annabel's and Lucy's mouths one more time, I don't know what I'll do. They think they're paying me a compliment! Being a dag—which no matter how many times they say it's a nice word, what I hear is an Aussie term that secretly means a smart, little nerd watching all the other kids around him sprouting! sprouting! sprouting!—it is a curse, not a compliment. It's not like that historic, tragic kind of Boston Red Sox curse where fans used to have to despair at Babe Ruth's dark-cloud ghost hovering over Fenway Park every season around play-off time, but at least those cursed BoSox players probably got cute girls. That's some consolation for having a curse, in my opinion.

I'm not girl-crazy like Annabel is boy-crazy. I am, simply, Lucy-crazy. In the year since I last saw her in New York, Lucy only got a million times prettier, and, uh, way more curvy. Wowza! And those baby blue eyes, the same color as the pool she so elegantly floats in, that sun-kissed blond hair, that beautiful exotic accent. She's "graayate!" Observing Lucy makes me want to clutch my fist to my heart and wail, as Bubbe might say, *Oh, I might be dying!*

When Lucy touched my feet in the pool this evening, I thought it was possible I could sink into the pool from happiness, except I didn't want to catch cold. Not like Lucy noticed. She spoke to me in that barking-orders tone, like she was Annabel as our incumbent eighth-grade class president: "Angus loves this book called *Aquarium Fishes of the World* and if he brings it to you, read it with him. You have to, okay?" Sure, Luce, whatever you say. In exchange, I'll hope drool isn't hanging from my mouth as I stare at you from afar as you and Annabel gush on about who else: BEN! *What do you think is Ben's favorite food? Let's make brownies for Ben! Everyone back in Melbourne says Ben is like the hottest guy in school now, like if he were in American high school he would be Homecoming King and Most Likely to Take Over the World with His Charm and Popularity* . . . Blah Blah BEN.

I sat at the computer and wondered if I could tap into some Mexican voodoo while I'm here in LA. The fundamental laws of nature prevent me from truly believing in that stuff, but I've seen the movie *Weird Science* at least a hundred times, so I know anything is possible. Hello, Google? Please find me a Mexican voodoo priestess who can conjure me some brawn this summer so I can become athletic like Lucy and she'll finally notice me—as more than just a dag. Refine search terms so that said voodoo won't have a bad catch to it, like Lucy finally falls for me but only for a single day and then she forgets all about me, or Annabel's worst nightmare comes true and she is forced to wear acid-washed jeans as penance for me playing with the dark arts. Google, my friend, my best friend—a plain reciprocated crush is all I'm asking. Is that hit so hard?

The computer speaker beeped the IM sound, and I saw that Annabel had hit me before Google had a chance to step up to the plate.

Wheaties, how bored were you reading The Book to Angus, anyway?

I typed back: *A lot. But did you know Angus can actually pronounce "Boleophthalmus Pectinirostris"—aka the Comb-Toothed Mudskipper (p. 127 of The Book)? Angus has the page marked, you should check the mudskipper dude out, the picture will scare you to . . .*

I didn't get a chance to finish or hit Send on the response before Annabel lobbed another question my way.

Do you think Harvey and Angelina are going to work things out?

Annabel and I never talk in person about what goes on between her mom and my dad, but somehow when we are apart, IMs seem to fill the space of those conversations between us.

I sent back: *I hope so.* I didn't add, *I hope so not only because I want Dad to be married and happy and I don't want be in LA any longer than I have to, but also because I like living with Angelina and the baby and you.* I didn't include that last part because I didn't want Annabel's head getting too big from the flattery.

She wrote back: *I hope so, too. This LA thing scares me. I don't think they've tried hard enough.*

So I pointed out: *Maybe it's not about trying hard enough, but simple statistics. Studies have shown that marriages that start out because the wife was preg . . .* only I hit Send by accident before I finished typing the sentence.

The response back was immediate: *No statistics, PLEASE! I will give baby Ariel a good night kiss from you. Seeyalater, Einstein.* And she signed off. She was probably right to sign off. The statistics are not encouraging.

I'd rather think about the statistical odds of me getting Lucy's attention all to myself. Dad doesn't have Angelina near him to try to make things right, but I'm here all summer for Lucy to notice. Probability-wise, the deck isn't that stacked against me.

I looked up from the computer monitor at the framed poster of Albert Einstein that Mom and Tia hung over the desk in this spare room that doubles as my bedroom when I visit over school breaks. The Einstein poster was like a slap in the face, taunting me: *Hey Wheaties, cheer up—geniuses are never appreciated in their own time. Actually, I was, but you probably won't be. Sorry, little fella!*

I prefer a different genius icon than Einstein. Since I've been bumped up to college-level summer reading assignments by the academic advisor at the high school I'll be starting in the fall, I've been studying the works of some of the great thinkers from way back. My favorite thinker is this Italian guy called Niccolo Machiavelli. I listened to the whole audio version of his treatise, *The Prince*, on the plane ride to LA. By the time the plane landed, I understood Machiavelli's indisputable truth: For the nation-state to survive and thrive, sometimes a prince has gotta be bad to protect the greater good. That Machiavelli guy's got it all over Einstein.

Lucy Lucy Lucy. There's a prince right in front of

you: ME! Wheaties the Prince must concoct a scheme to expose Ben as a brainless jock unworthy of the girls' attention. A scheme will come to me; it has to. As Machiavelli said, "There is nothing more difficult to take in hand, more perilous to conduct, or more uncertain in its success, than to take the lead in the introduction of a new order to things."

Here's where being a dag can actually work in my favor. Lucy and Annabel think I'm so good and sweet, innocent little daggy Wheaties. They won't even see my Ben scheme coming! That's because, as this Machiavelli dude will tell you, the appearance of virtue is more important than true virtue, which is pointless. "For the great majority of mankind are satisfied with appearances, as though they were realities, and are often more influenced by the things that seem than by those that are."

"Knock, knock," I heard Mom's voice say. When she could have just knocked, instead of saying it. I turned around from the computer, where I sat building a program to calculate Ben's downfall. Mom stood just outside the room, wearing her lawyer uniform—dark blue power suit and navy pumps, with her curly strawberry hair that's just like mine pulled back into a tight lawyer-lady bun.

"Hi . . . Mom," I said, even though my first instinct was to call her Debbie like Annabel calls her mom Angelina. But calling my mother Debbie felt even more personal than calling her Mom, so I didn't. I don't know her well enough to call her Debbie. Every time I see her, it's like meeting her all over again. It's the same impersonal feeling like when she takes me to her office and introduces me around and the people there will be all, "Oh, Debbie, we didn't even realize you *had* a son! He looks just like you!"

"Alan," Mom stated. She stepped into the room, but only barely, like she was awkward being in her own home. "Tia said you two had a great day at Venice Beach with Annabel and her family." She stepped in a little closer, peering at me. "Did you get sun on your face?" *No, Mom, that's the little red zits bursting on my face in time for Lucy to see. Thanks for asking, Mom.*

When I didn't answer, she said, "So. How is your father?"

HOW DO YOU THINK HE IS, MOM?!?!? His new wife and baby have left him for the summer, his business is a mess until the sale goes through—if it goes through, and he doesn't think I know this, but he also has to sell our summer house in order to maintain the mortgage on the big new apartment he bought when he married Angelina. Dad doesn't even want me around this summer until he can get all this mess fixed up, and I'm probably the closest person to him!

"He's fine," I muttered. Focusing on developing a scheme to sabotage Ben is much more pleasant than thinking of Dad all alone in our apartment back in New York, figuring out his life, without me there to help him.

"Do you think he and Angelina will work things

out?" Mom asked. I can't help but be curious if she asked because she's afraid Dad and Angelina won't work things out and then I'll want to live with her, or because Mom actually cares how Dad might be feeling. If she had more practice being a regular mom, she'd know she's not supposed to ask me questions like that. Angelina will let me talk about anything with her—but when it comes to how she and Dad feel about each other, Angelina leaves me out of it. For which I thank her.

"I don't know," I said. "I guess so." I want Dad and Angelina to work things out, but after spending this past evening at the pool with Angelina's ex and his family, watching Angelina and Penny laughing with each other, and the assorted kids all blending together and having fun family time, it's hard not to suspect that Angelina is happier here than she was in New York with Dad. My own mom is happier here in LA with Tia than she was back in New York, obviously, but I couldn't see Mom being open to making friends with her ex's new wife, or playing with the new wife's kids, the way Angelina does with Penny and her family, and which I think is pretty nice. Angelina and Jack might not get along that great themselves, but they make it all work because that's how much they love Annabel. I don't see Mom ever doing that for me. Annabel is worried that Angelina and Dad haven't tried hard enough? She should spend more time with *my* mom. I don't think it occurs to Mom to try at all with me.

"Love is hard," Mom pronounced. Huh? Was Mom expressing sympathetic support for what Dad's going through or spouting wisdom from the fortune-cookie paper she held in her hand? "Come to the dining room. I brought home some Chinese takeout." I don't know how I can be so small considering I ate a huge dinner at Jack and Penny's and still, my stomach grumbled at the suggestion of Chinese food. I got up from the computer to follow Mom into the dining room, where Tia had set the table with candles and flowers like we had a real celebration going instead of midnight food from a box.

Tia must not realize that love *is* hard. She should study Machiavelli about it, not her boy Dr. Phil—she'd learn a lot more. Sayeth *my* boy Machiavelli: "Love endures by a bond which men, being scoundrels, may break whenever it serves their advantage to do so; but fear is supported by the dread of pain, which is ever present."

Watch your back, Ben-boy.

Chapter 9

Ben

Miss Shouty made us late getting to Penny's house. We were stopped at a red light on Sunset Boulevard, but Miss Shouty couldn't just sit still through the light, noooo. She had to hop out of the car to buy a star map from a guy sitting in a lawn chair on the street corner. She hadn't finished inspecting the map when the light turned green, so all the drivers in back of us honked their car horns and yelled at her from their open car-door windows. "Stop holding up traffic!" "Get a move on, lady!" Honk hoooooonk.

Things move fast here in America. There's no time even to buy a star map. It's not like Dad or I even wanted one, but why would Miss Shouty care about that?

The honking and yelling didn't rile Miss Shouty one bit. It encouraged her. The noise inspired her to take an extra long time taking out her money to pay for the map, and once she'd paid for the map, she slooooowly counted the change. She then placed her hand on her hip and shouted at the long line of cars behind us, "WAIT A BLOODY MINUTE, WILL YA, HEY?" She made a rather rude hand gesture at all the cars behind us waiting to pass through the green light, but it was an Australian gesture that's not famous here in America, so who knows if the other drivers even knew they'd been told off by her hand. All they would have seen is a tall, tanned, bleached blonde with croc-leather skin, making strange hand signals at them instead of jumping back into her car so she could move out of their way.

The light had turned back to red by the time she got back into the passenger seat of our car. I sank further down into the backseat and placed my hands over my ears to drown out the honks and Miss Shouty's yelling at Dad, who hadn't said a word. "PATRICK! CAN YOU BELIEVE THESE RUDE PEOPLE? CAN'T EVEN RELAX A MOMENT SO A TOURIST CAN BUY A STAR MAP! WELCOME TO AMERICA— NOT REALLY!"

Miss Shouty does not know how to speak in a normal tone. For her shouting *is* normal, which would worry me except I've met some of her other family, and they all shout too. It's not just her. It's some genetic disorder passed from one shouty generation to the next. The shouting only happens to be more

103

annoying on her than on them because the rest of her family are not dating my dad and forcing me to "vacation" with them.

It's been a long trip, made longer since Miss Shouty insisted we keep our true arrival date in LA a secret. Dad told Penny we could all get together anytime during the week we're visiting Southern California. What he didn't mention is we've already been here a week because Miss Shouty insisted we have time for ourselves before we can visit with Dad's ex-wife and her family. I'm under strict orders not to mention anything about our few days in San Francisco, the drive down the coast to the Hearst Castle, or our two days in San Diego. Who'd want to mention that time, anyway? Every place we've been so far has been BORING. All we've done is wait in queues: hours waiting for the boat ride to Alcatraz in San Francisco; hours of waiting in traffic on the drive down the coast because a truck had overturned and deposited a cargo load of peanut butter across the highway; and more waiting to check into our hotels or to be seated at Applebee's, whose menu incidentally has not very much to do with apples.

But all those lines turned out to be the opening act for the mother of all queues, that being the horror that is Disneyland, where Miss Shouty has waited a lifetime to go. Great, I'm so excited to wait an hour in line to go ride through Space Mountain, or wait another hour for a two-minute roller-coaster ride, all scheduled around the particular Miss Shouty waiting time: to queue up for her many loo stops or wait for her to get her picture taken with Goofy or waiting for her to file a formal complaint after Mickey Mouse's hands strayed a little too far down her bum when she asked him for a hug.

I can't *wait* to go home.

Back home in Melbourne, Miss Shouty doesn't live with us—*yet*—so at least I get some time to myself without her there. Here, I'm trapped with her. I didn't know what Dad saw in her before our big trip to America, and after a week of traveling with her, I know even less. So she's really nice about doing his washing, and ironing his shirts the way he likes, and she brings him hot lunches when he's working, and who wouldn't like a good meal delivered to them, but beyond that, I can't figure out her appeal to him.

She's not even that great-looking. If a bloke is going to put up with all that shouting from his lady, he should at least get a babe. Miss Shouty owns a tanning salon. I reckon she has an attractive figure, which apparently she must want the whole world to see, as her wardrobe is mostly tight blouses and short skirts, but her tanning-salon leather skin looks like it should be in a horror movie, and incidentally, horror movie is probably her cosmetic inspiration. She wears gobs of hideous pancake makeup on her face, with white shadow on her eyes that, set against her dark tanned skin, gives her eyes a domino look.

Dad's a shy guy, so maybe it's not that he sees something in her but that she's simply chosen him, and he's too polite not to go along with someone who wants him. He's not a guy who would put himself out there to find a non-shouty lady on his own. Dad and I were better off before he had to go and get claimed by a girlfriend.

No one ever thought he'd date again after Mum passed away, but then he met Penny in a support group, and that was all right. Penny was nice—and polite. She took care of us, and I liked her kids and they liked me. Maybe it was all too nice. Penny and Dad never held hands or kissed or did any of those couple things. Their marriage was more like, "Patrick, the bathtub drain is backed up again, would you mind terribly fixing that?" and "Yes, Penny, I'll be sure to fix that. Would it be possible for you to pick up Ben after his footy game on Friday? I'll be tied up at work, completing the renovation job at the St. Kilda house. Thanks ever so much."

Dad and Penny didn't last a year together, but Dad and I have been fine on our own ever since, until Miss Shouty had to come along. She hired him to repair some storm damage on the roof of her house, but as soon as she found out he was single, all of a sudden she needed new tiles in her kitchen. By the time Dad upgraded the electrical wiring in her house, she was a permanent fixture back at our house. Life lesson: If you're going to be a housing contractor, don't take odd jobs for shouty, single women. Those jobs can spiral out of control.

Dad has saved for years to take us on a trip to America. He's been talking up the vacation like he would be visiting the promised land. Only, he didn't mention there would be a Miss Shouty involved, all these years he's been dreaming of this vacation. Ten years Dad has been tucking away bits of cash so we could have this adventure and guess what? I'd rather be back home playing footy with my mates at the oval, or even doing school work.

I might be a quiet guy, and I might not get the top marks at school, but I've got me a life plan. I reckon I'll become a pro footy player like everyone expects, but footy players have limited careers, like child actors. So I'll make my name as a pro player first, then I'll move over to the business side, rather than coach. I want more. After my amazing but short footy career, I'll get a business degree at university. Eventually I'll purchase my own footy-team franchise and then use that team as the launch pad for introducing Aussie-rules footy to the rest of the world. One day, Aussie footy will dominate world sports like stupid soccer does now, and all because of me and my plan. You're welcome, world.

"WHERE'S GEORGE CLOONEY'S HOUSE!" shouted you-know-who as Dad inched the car along a posh street that appeared to be all shrubs, tall fences, and fancy cars parked at the curb. "PATRICK, YOU

CAN BARELY SEE THE HOUSE FROM THE STREET. THE STAR MAP IS FALSE ADVERTIS-ING—YOU CAN'T SEE ANY OF THESE HOUSES WITH ALL THIS SHRUBBERY!"

From the backseat, I took my headphones off. Not even Green Day could drown out Miss Shouty. I reminded Dad, "I think Penny was expecting us about an hour ago?" When Miss Shouty bought the star map, she didn't realize that houses on the map are much farther apart than they appear on the map. She made Dad drive totally out of our way just to find Rod Stewart's house, whoever bloody Rod Stewart is!

Dad finally remembered he could make decisions independently of HER. "We'd better get over to Penny's," he said. "No more star-mapping for today."

When we got to Penny's house, it felt like a real home after the week of crap hotels and long car trips. The house had normal furniture instead of hotel fur-niture, with an eating nook off the kitchen where she'd laid out a plate of Tim Tam biscuits with some bread and Vegemite spread for us. She even had proper Australian cordial for us to drink instead of the too-sweet juice drinks found here in America. Why couldn't *she* still be Dad's lady?

Only Penny and her baby greeted us, as the rest of her family were out. I was disappointed as I really could have used a dose of Angus. I had been looking forward to taking the little tike out to the backyard for us to kick the footy around for a while and escape Miss

Shouty's shrill voice—to use Angus to get a vacation from my "vacation."

Here's an interesting way to get Miss Shouty to shut up. Introduce her to Dad's ex-wife. I'd never seen her so quiet as we sat around the table at Penny's. "Ben!" Penny said. "Angus and the girls can't wait to see you! Although you'll please excuse us if things are a little tense at lunch this afternoon. Jack and his daughter had a little quarrel earlier, but I'm hoping they'll have calmed down by then. He's out with Lucy and Angus, picking up some ice cream for us all. Just look at you, Ben! How tall are you now, anyway?"

"He's six foot," Dad said. "You should see the size of our grocery bill."

"Tell me about it," Penny said. "We've got three children living here, one and a half stepchildren if you count Wheaties coming round, and Jack's clients seem to drop in all the time as well. The grocery expenses are outrageous."

Ah, just like old times between Dad and Penny: a perfectly boring, even-toned conversation. Of course Miss Shouty had to ruin that. She admired the little girl on Penny's lap and whined, "I want a baby . . ."

Dad's answer was a strange hybrid of yes and no. "N'yah," he squirmed.

GOOD GOD, WHEN CAN WE GO HOME!

Lucky for Dad that we heard a door slam from the front of the house, and Lucy and Angus ran into the kitchen to greet us.

LUCY! My eyes could possibly be gouged out like in an ancient Greek play for noticing my former stepsister the way I did, in the not-former-family way. Last time I saw her was in Melbourne when she and her stepsister snuck away from Sydney. What a difference a year and half, and a new country, have made for her.

"Hi Ben!" she said. I forgot how she is all bubbly and sweet. "We're so excited you're finally here! We have all this fun stuff planned for us to do this week!"

"Who's we?" I asked.

"Me and Annabel, of course!"

Oh yeah, Annabel. We used to chat online a bit after we first met but that dropped off—the time difference between Melbourne and New York made it one big bother. Annabel is memorable to me not for our online conversations, but because live in the flesh, she was the first girl I ever kissed. That seems like ages ago. I'm fifteen and a half now and have gotten a lot more experience since.

I was never raised around girls—it's mostly been me and my Dad my whole life, with no aunts or girl cousins to balance our family out. I don't claim to understand anything about females, yet somehow, girls have discovered me. I can be a quiet guy like Dad, but I'm not as timid. Dad doesn't know about the girls I've gotten to know lately, and I used to tell him everything. I haven't even told my own mates—I don't need to brag. I'm keeping the girl thing under the radar. Right now I seem to be the "go-to" guy for the older punk-rock chicks, the sixteen- and seventeen-year-old variety who I think are just lovely with their pouty faces of spiky piercings and goth lippy colors. The punk-rock chicks think making out with a footy type is the ultimate in rebellion, yet they're also repulsed by their attraction to a sporty fellow, so they don't want to be seen in public with him, which works out perfectly. I get the make-out sessions without being claimed by a grating girlfriend. Who's the dumb spunk now? And, the punk-rock girls are GREAT kissers, much better than the popular, pretty girls who I find to be most enthusiastic to be kissed, but lacking technique—or maybe just lacking experience.

I could feel my face flush from the unnatural thoughts I was all of a sudden having of bubbly, new California girl Lucy transformed into a punk-rock Melbourne girl, with black smudge-lined eyes and tiger streaks of black and copper through her blond hair, so I was grateful to feel Angus tug on my hand. "C'mon," he said. "Let's go play."

"Where's the footy?" I asked. Yes! Finally, something decent to do.

"No, silly," Angus said. He plopped a blue book that weighed as much as a small free weight at the gym into my hand. The book was called *Aquarium Fishes of the World*. "Come to my room and we can read this book, hey Ben?"

Bloody miserable vacation.

Chapter 10

Annabel

I knew eventually the LA perfect thing would break down and the arguing would get started. I just didn't expect the fight would be between me and Dad. Jack and Angelina, Lucy and Angus, me and that ever-present Maurice guy—if I were a Vegas oddsmaker, these would have been the pairs I would have bet on for some smackdowns. But Dad and me? We don't get to see each other nearly enough, so it's almost like we work extra hard to get along when we are together. But now that we're seeing each other every day like a regular dad and daughter, somehow he thinks he can go all official father figure on me instead of temporary dad.

I don't like it.

On the Saturday morning of the big day, Jack stopped by our rental house on his way up the canyon for a morning hike with Lucy and Angus. I was planning to go on the hike with them, but then I decided I needed more time assembling my outfit and doing my hair in preparation for Ben's arrival that afternoon. Dad said I looked fine, but he wasn't going to bother debating the issue with a fourteen-year-old girl. Talk about ignorant—I was wearing sweats! What did he know? Dad promised they would stop by again on their way down the canyon to pick me up, and we could all go back to his house together to wait for Ben, Patrick, and Patrick's girlfriend. Simple, right? Where's the drama there?

First, Dad had to deposit Maurice at our house on his way up the canyon. The big troll beast came into our house, and the baby crawled right over to where he'd plopped down on the sofa, while Maurice cooed at her, "Who's your daddy?" That's comedy? After only a few weeks here, Ariel does love Maurice like he could be her papa; she's not old enough to know better. The baby didn't mind at all when Papa Smurfbeast crouched down on the floor alongside her and tried to get her to run lines with him from the script he was holding. Lucy and Angus laughed hysterically at Maurice's attempts to get an innocent baby to play the part of Maurice's dad, a grumpy old man with a heart of gold, while I glared at Jack.

I walked away in disgust and Jack followed behind me. He came inside my bedroom, uninvited. He said, "You know, you're very rude to Maurice. You don't say 'hello' or even acknowledge him. Aside from him being my biggest client, he's also my friend. I don't appreciate your attitude, young lady." No good discussion is about to happen when a parent drops "young lady" into their sentence.

Attitude schmattitude.

What could I possibly say? *Yo, Dad, why do you keep encouraging your so-called friend and client to use your ex for his acting coach? Maurice has gotten to the point where he can't even rehearse without my mother being present. Do you really think Maurice's intentions are purely professional?*

I plugged in my flatiron and sat down at the vanity table. I looked at Jack through the mirror and mumbled, "Sorry." My fingers were crossed on my lap because I totally wasn't sorry. But I didn't need a lecture ruining the beauty energy I was accumulating in anticipation of preparing to see BEN!!!!!! *Om* to the highest power.

The mumbled "sorry," even if I totally didn't mean it, seemed to satisfy him. Jack left my room. The big day wasn't off to a great start, but a fight had been averted. For then.

I had spent days picking the right skirt and top and trying on loads of different jewelry to get just the right effect. I was long over the notion of a simple Gap skirt and Blunnie boots to wear for Ben; two weeks in practically-naked-people LA had inspired a more frisky choice of clothing. While Jack and The Steps were out hiking, I invested a good hour and a half into getting dressed, straightening my hair with a flatiron, putting on false eyelashes instead of mascara (which is no easy task, believe me), and applying the light-pink eye shadow and lip gloss colors that Angelina had preapproved.

The rule is, until I am sixteen, I have to get Mom's approval for the makeup I wear. The approval is silly because I would never go tacky overboard with that stuff—*subtle* rules my cosmetic philosophy. But the approval thing makes her feel all proper Mommy-Fresh4U, I guess, so I go along with her because I'm generous that way. Bubbe says it's important to choose your battles, and eye shadow and lipstick colors shouldn't be mine with Mom. I'm saving up for important battles, like a later curfew and an increased allowance. Besides, Angelina's taste is so similar to my own that we don't disagree on makeup unless I wear blue eyeliner on the inside of my eye rim. She says the rim eyeliner is unhygienic and also very '80s, which just goes to show my mother's one true fashion challenge. She has good taste but no artistic vision—she doesn't take fashion risks. The compromise we've worked out is I put the eyeliner on when she's not around and wash it off before I see her again. She never knows, and everyone wins.

Dad's all into the fact that I am a good student and seriously motivated, so he should have been proud of the superior work ethic I put into my look for the big day. Beauty takes a lot of time and concentration! And the end result, in my opinion, was perfect. I admired myself in the full-length mirror, imagining that Ben might also admire my short white skirt, Pucci knock-off psychedelic-pink-print halter top, and beaded strappy sandals that matched my raspberry-colored toenails. I'm horrified by the full-on-naked LA look, though, so while I wore a low-ride skirt that exposed my waist and hips, the skirt's length was not ultra-short. It fell to a few inches above my knees, and I had rubbed self-tanning lotion on my legs since the skirt was showing off bare leg. The trick with the halter top was it fell loose around the chest area but was cut high up my torso. In combination with the skirt riding well below my waist, the outfit exposed my long tummy and narrow hips, and distracted the eye from the complete lack of cleavage underneath the loose halter. Thanks, Gwen Stefani—you're a musical icon *and* a flat-chested girl's fashion inspiration!

I had the radio going as I dressed and put on my face, and the music had put me in a great mood by the time Jack came back with Lucy and Angus to get me. I don't know which upset him first—my outfit, or that I was dancing Beyoncé's *uh-oh uh-oh uh-oh* moves from her classic *Crazy In Love* video in the full-length mirror—but Dad flipped out when he came into my room and saw me.

"NO!" he yelled, which startled my happy-anticipation mood because he never yells. "CHANGE. NOW!"

I laughed because I honestly thought he was joking. Men don't appreciate how much work a girl can put into choosing an outfit, fixing her hair, and applying makeup. Who was he to tell me what to wear? I never realized Jack thought he had any say in what I wear. I never even thought he noticed!

"Yeah, right," I said. I grabbed my fake Louis Vuitton little shoulder bag from the bed, ready to head down the street and toward my Ben destiny.

I walked past him, but he grabbed my arm to stop me! "I'm not kidding," he said. "No fourteen-year-old daughter of mine is going out dressed like that." He looked over at Lucy, standing in the hallway outside my room, who had just mouthed "perfect" and made the A-OK sign at me when Dad's back was turned to her. "That goes for you, too, Lucy!"

Lucy's jaw dropped. "What do I have to do with it?" she said. "Besides, I think Annabel looks great."

"You're also fourteen," Jack said. "You would." He closed my bedroom door on her and turned back to me, pointing his finger in my face. What lame-TV dad sitcom did he get *that* move from? "Annabel, under no circumstances can you wear that outfit, especially with Ben being at the house this afternoon. Do you realize how you look?"

"Fantastic?" I asked.

"Fantastic for a hoo . . ." Dad started to answer, but then Angelina popped into my room, and he stopped whatever he was about to say. He'd better not have been about to call me a hoochie mama!

"What's going on?" Angelina asked. Mom hadn't

seen my outfit yet. "Oh, honey, you look beautiful!" she said.

Jack threw his arms up in the air. "SHE. IS. NOT. WEARING. THAT. I swear, Angelina, do you have any sense at all? What kind of message is that outfit sending? Think about it."

Here's the weirdest part. Usually when Jack baits Angelina, she'll fight back to the death. But instead, she appraised my outfit once again and sided with him! "Maybe Jack's right, sweetie. Maybe . . ."

"NOOOOOOOOO!!!!!!!!!!!!" I screamed, totally fed up. "YOU HAVE NO RIGHT TO TELL ME WHAT TO WEAR!"

Jack said, "I have every right. It's called being your father. I'm going to the grocery store with Lucy and Angus. I'll look forward to seeing you at the house later, after you've changed into an age-appropriate outfit. A ladylike one. Listen up because here's the new rule. Bare legs or bare stomach—choose one because you can't have both."

He stormed out with Angelina following behind him. I kicked the bedroom door so hard behind them that it got a small dent from my spiked, metal sandal heel. I jumped onto the bed: FURIOUS. I wiped away the tears from my eyes, which, unfortunately, rubbed off the fake eyelashes on one side, after all that work. HOW DARE HE?!?!?!?!? Why was Jack trying to sabotage the one day I had looked forward to? He's old and withered and has NO IDEA how important and hard it is for a girl to look good. And EXCUSE ME, but he's the one who moved to Australia and had a whole new family without me, so who was HE to tell me what to wear, anyway?

The radio played one of those angry punk-girl songs. I don't really like that kind of music, but in this moment, the p.o.'d girl's wail actually calmed me down. The song helped me realize that my hopes for a loud and proud fashion statement might not be entirely lost. I could trade in my NY-pretty-girl-chic-meets-Gwen Stefani look into a Gwen Stefani-as-angry-punk-girl look. I could still appear good for Ben *and* get back at Jack.

Chapter 11

Lucy

his·tri·on·ics: *n.* 1. *(used with a pl. verb)* Theatrical arts or performances; 2. *(used with a sing. or pl. verb)* exaggerated emotional behavior calculated for effect.
Oh, now I get it!

If I look in the crystal ball of Annabel's future, I could totally see that she may ultimately toss her designer ambitions aside to become a fashionista magazine editrix. Her magazine could be called *Histrionic* and will spawn a major new anger-management, feminine fashion trend. She'll write columns like "Dress to Diss: Basic Black Bondage That Only a Father Could Hate."

Who knew Annabel (or Angelina, more likely) even owned an old, beat-up, black leather motorcycle-biker-babe jacket, or that Annabel owned a short black skirt with a zipper riding high up the side? Um, *really* short skirt—she definitely took up Dad on his rule to choose between either bare legs or a bare stomach. I never thought a day would come when Annabel would want to borrow both my Doc Martens black boots and my black turtleneck top. The boots are old and worn-out, and while the black top wasn't made from the dreaded percale fabric, it was still a poly-cotton Target blend Annabel normally shuns. So much for her supposed high standards. And I never suspected the large suitcase of hair and beauty products she lugged from NYC contained cans of temporary orange and black hair spray. Even a crystal ball couldn't have helped me predict that Annabel, of all people, would streak her hair with orange and black spray or that she would clump strands of hair into messy piles hanging from her head.

Also, green lipstick with red lipliner? Pumpkin-colored hair and a Christmas-themed mouth was the last face I ever expected to see on Annabel. At least the holiday-themed face still had the sulk, so I knew she was still my Annabel under there. For a minute, as I inspected her completed fashion statement, I worried she'd been kidnapped and replaced at our house with a punk-girl clone. But the sulk made the outfit. Well done, girl!

Annabel wanted to make a grand entrance, so she IM'ed me in advance to wait in my bedroom until she snuck over. I was there when she tapped on the window from the ground. She crawled through my window and got ready in my room without Dad or Ben even knowing she was here. I knew she wanted to irritate Dad with the outfit, but she must have wanted to get back at Angelina, too. "I thought you weren't allowed to wear black eyeliner inside your eye," I said. The eyeliner was not only lined inside the rim of her eye, but lined above and below her eyes as well. I don't wear makeup. Too much bother.

"*Blue* eyeliner," Annabel said. "Mom never said anything against *black* eyeliner." She adjusted her shoulders. "This jacket is SO heavy. I used to think these jackets were tacky, but now I have a whole new level of respect for girls who wear them. They suffer for their fashion art. Got a smoke?"

"You don't smoke!" Annabel was the person who had once talked *me* out of trying to smoke.

"Of course I don't. Do you know what that stuff does to your lungs and how bad it makes your hair smell? I just want the box visible in the jacket pocket, like an accessory." Wow, she's good.

"Mum keeps a sneak box of cigarettes and candy in the basement near the washing machine; she doesn't think I know about them."

"Go," Annabel ordered.

I knew I shouldn't be involved in her scheme, but I couldn't help myself. Nothing interesting ever happens around here, and that's why we count on Annabel to shake things up.

I found Angus sitting on the washing machine

when I stepped down into the basement. "What are you doing all alone here?" I asked him.

"Having a think," he said.

"About what?"

He shrugged. "Dunno."

Josephine Snickercross suspected he did know, and she had to find out. Angus alone in the basement when his hero Ben was visiting all the way from Australia wasn't right.

I sat up on the dryer next to him. Josephine knew the best way to Angus's heart. *"Nemacheilus fasciatus?"*

Angus's brooding face relaxed a little and he let out a small giggle. *"Nemacheilus fasciatus:* aquarium fish from Sumatra, Java, and Borneo that work best when given a tank of their own because they choose and defend their own territories . . ."

Then at the same time, Angus and I both sang out, *"Likes worms and other live foods, but not a fussy eater!"* I have no idea why, but this fact about *Nemacheilus fasciatus* from p. 479 of *Aquarium Fishes of the World* has been cracking us up since before Mum met Jack.

Our laugh didn't distract Angus from his Serious Thought, though. "Was Josephine Snickercross really just a dugong?" he wanted to know. "Because Ben told me mermaids aren't really real. He said in the olden days, sailors who had been at sea for long periods of time claimed they saw creatures with the head and body of a woman and a fish's tail. They thought the creatures were mermaids, but really they were just dugongs. Ben told me dugongs are shark-shaped rare sea mammals with rounded faces, who hold their bodies upright in the water, so they look like they're human. So maybe Josephine isn't real, but a dugong."

Who knew Ben had a factoid brain lurking under that lovely athletic exterior? Ben the clever footy boy and Annabel the clothes snob painting herself as a rebel girl for the day? Those two and their mixed-up identities must be meant for each other, like fate or something.

"Want to know a secret?" I asked Angus. So long as Angus still believes in Santa Claus, he shall also believe in Josephine Snickercross.

"YES!" he said.

"First you have to promise to stop saying bad American words you learned at school." I've been waiting for my opportunity to call Angus out on expressions like "yo mama" without it seeming like a big-sister lecture. I love us living in America, but the things he learns in school here are shocking.

"Okay." Nice—that win was easy!

"Josephine is part dugong, part human. An interspecies. You'd never read about her kind in a book because they are like a secret society."

"Oh," Angus said, nodding his head, like *of course Josephine was a mixed breed from a secret society, that explains everything.* The Josephine matter settled, Angus decided, "You should marry Ben so then he could live with us. That would be graayate!"

Just what are they teaching at his school in America to make him think I'm old enough to be married— and to my former stepbrother! I'm glad for Annabel and her crush because it seems very important to her, but I'd like to know why there even has to be an assumption that everyone should be coupled up? When I hear Angelina on her mobile phone arguing with Harvey while Maurice is making eyes at her, or watch Mum and Patrick in awkward conversation while Dad kicks the footy in the backyard with Ben, or find myself fixing a Coke for Tia in our kitchen since she's taking Wheaties around because his mum is always working, I can't help but think that coupling up doesn't necessarily lead to happily ever after. Heartache and loss jump on the party bus, too. Annabel's in this mad rush for a boyfriend, but me? I'd like to just be me for a while. Despite today's drama, everything is pretty good in our family right now after not being good for a very long time, and I plan to enjoy that—on my own and crush-free.

I told Angus, "Sorry, champ. Ben's practically related. And we don't like each other that way. It would be like incest." Oops! Here I was trying to call Angus out on using bad words, and now look at the language I was letting slip in front of him! Naughty, Lucy.

Angus announced, "But incest is best!" Bloody American school where he learns these things!

I kicked my leg against his on the machine. "WHAT!!!!!!!!!!!!!!!" I said. "You don't even know what incest is." I only came to the basement to get Mum's sneak box of cigs (for Annabel) and lollies (for me), and now I find Angus down here more disturbed than Annabel upstairs.

"I do too."

"What is it?"

"When insects have a party. Right?"

I knew better than to laugh at him. "Right," I said. The party-bus brakes could be slammed right now on giving Angus information that could help him grow up any more quickly than he is already. Although I do look forward to the day when Angus is grown enough to stroll the supermarket aisles alone without Mum making me hold his hand and take him where I wander, because I like to go to the freezer section and rapidly open and close the ice cream freezer doors to feel the spots of chill blast my face, but that's my private thing, shhhh.

Looking after Angus can be annoying, but the truth is, I like him just the way he is: as a kid.

Chapter 12

Ben

I like all these sets of families Lucy and her stepsister have here in LA because at least with them, if one person bothers you, there are loads of others around to entertain you. If any of those kids got trapped with a Miss Shouty, I reckon they could go over someone else's house. That's just what The Punk Girl I Kissed Once and I did after Miss Shouty got too annoying at dinner at Jack and Penny's house. We went to that girl's place for a second dinner after the first one turned out to be lousy.

Now that Miss Shouty has waited a lifetime to visit America and is finally realizing her dream thanks to the convergence of Dad's savings account, her begging for a vacation abroad, and my school holiday, her dinner conversation consisted of her shouting on about how great Australia is. We sat through an appetizer, salad, and main course with Miss Shouty regaling us with Aussie info too boring to repeat. Someone should write an etiquette guide for traveling shouty women, something like *Down Under Vacationers Going Up Over for Dummies*. If Miss Shouty had any sense, she'd know that first of all, she's in a foreign country supposedly learning about a new culture instead of longing for her own. Second, Jack's lived in Australia and Penny is Australian, so I think it's safe to say the two of them already knew all about Australia. The peculiar part was, after Angus and the little one were sent to bed and the adults had gone through two bottles of wine, Jack and Penny laughed along with Dad and Miss Shouty and her rantings like they were old college mates having a sorry old reunion. Sickening.

Before arriving in LA, I honestly hadn't much remembered the punk girl at the dinner table except for that long-ago kiss, but I easily took notice of her this evening. I recalled her being pretty-perky, the popular type of nice girl, but now she was all pouty and pretty-punk. More in her favor, she appeared to find the scene with Dad and Miss Shouty, and Jack and Penny, as revolting as I did. Instead of eating, she must have had an eye-twitching problem, because her eyes jumped from glaring at her father to staring at me. Although with all that black smudgy stuff around her eyes, I couldn't tell whether she really had eye-twitch issues or if maybe she was temporarily blinded or dumbstruck when she looked at me. But she ended up providing my escape route, so what did I care?

Her mum rang the house as Jack and Penny served ice cream for dessert. The Rocky Road flavor looked mighty tempting, but I still hungered for real food after the California-cuisine vegetable dinner. I'm a growing boy, I need much more nourishment. But because of Angus and the punk girl, who are vegetarians, Jack and Penny didn't serve meat, and because of an afternoon with Angus and his boring fish encyclopedia, I hungered for some seafood something bad.

How fantastic to me, then, when the punk girl chatted with her mum on the phone and then told her dad, "Mom and Maurice are having sushi up the street at our house. And they bought a cake because they're celebrating your oh-so important client Maurice's show getting a whadyacallit—a midseason pickup. Tia is dropping Wheaties over to spend the night, and Mom wants me to come home."

"So go," Jack said, sounding curt for a bloke who struck me as being a great guy. Angus wouldn't play footy with me, but Jack had spent a good hour with me, kicking the ball around in the backyard while Penny, Dad, and Miss Shouty fixed dinner together. The guy is talented, too: He could throw and catch the ball while chasing a two-year-old girl around the yard.

Instead of hanging up the phone after getting her dad's permission, Lucy's stepsister paused a moment, like she was gathering her strength to spit out whatever she had to say. When she did speak, it was very quickly, like she had to get it out before she lost her nerve. Her hand over the telephone mouthpiece, she added, "Mom said she'd like Ben to walk me home because it's getting dark and also that Ben is invited to hang out for a while with us if he wants, until his dad is ready to go back to their hotel tonight."

I don't know if it's an American trait, but she talked about me without looking at me, like I wasn't sitting right there at the table and might want to have some say in the matter. And what was up with Penny and Lucy all of a sudden looking very intently down at their bowls of ice cream and appearing to be smothering giggles?

Whatever I missed, I didn't care. Sushi! And cake! Ben the growing boy: STILL HUNGRY!

I don't know why that simple invitation needed any negotiation, but Jack took the phone from his daughter's hand; the black nail varnish and the metal rings on it looked most appealing, reminding me of certain older girls back in Melbourne, except the fingers on her hand weren't red from picking and biting. Jack excused himself to the kitchen. Obviously his dinner with Miss Shouty had taught him how to adjust his voice to shriek tone when talking on the phone with his daughter's mum.

When Jack came back into the dining room, he sighed as if he'd lost whatever the spat was with the ex. Jack said to me, "Ben, I'd appreciate if you could walk my daughter home. It's just a few blocks up the hill. Her mother, who's decided to be the big hero of the day, has a friend over who she thinks you'd be interested in meeting, and they're a person short for a decent Pictionary game. Allegedly." He looked at his punk-girl daughter. "Annabel, I'll come pick Ben up in exactly an hour." He turned to his Aussie daughter, sounding a little sarcastic when he spoke to her. "Lucy, I told Angelina I knew you would feel bad if you were left out, so you can go too." Now he smiled, like he'd scored at least one small victory in whatever game was being played out that I didn't get AT ALL.

Lucy has a sweet voice so she didn't sound whiny when she said, "I don't think I should go with them, Dad. I . . . um . . . got a headache from eating this ice cream too fast."

Jack said, "You're fine. Go on with them."

"But Dad! I don't feel well. I have . . . you know . . ." Lucy looked back down at her bowl of ice cream, which had indeed turned her face red.

"You're fine, Luce," Jack said. "Now go along with your sister and Ben."

Lucy slapped her hand down on the table. She said, "Your Honor, I plead guilty to . . . uh . . . feminine troubles! I'm really not feeling well, Dad. I think I need to go to bed. Mum, where did you leave the ibuprofen?" Lucy got up from the table and sprinted toward her room. Penny rushed to clear dishes from the table, as something in the kitchen demanded she let out some laughs in there. Jack stayed at the table rather than follow his wife or his daughter from the dining room. I would have too if I were him, what with the mention of "feminine troubles." Blokes know not to go there.

I must remember for any future travel guide I write to warn the naïve antipodean wanderer that dinner-time rituals in America are very bizarre.

On the walk up the hill to her house, Annabel and I didn't have much to say to each other at first. Our lips touched once in a random incident on the opposite side of the world, in a whole other universe to the one we stood in now. What were we supposed to do a year and a half later—have some conversation?

After the week with Miss Shouty, I rather enjoyed the silence as we strolled up a very steep hill with tall trees and some lovely homes and some plain homes next to one another, like very schizophrenic architecture. In our neighborhood in Melbourne, the small Victorian houses are built in uniform rows, with small gardens and with iron lace on the gates and windows to give the homes flavor. Here, the flavor was all over the place: large forest trees shooting up in the air, flower beds on some lawns and rocks and Zen-like bushes on others, shrubbery hiding cottage houses, which were built next to stately near-mansions. I liked that finally, free of Miss Shouty, I could look around at how different LA looked from any place I've ever seen. Traveling to strange places might not be so bad, if you took Miss Shouty out of the equation.

I reckon Annabel wasn't paying attention to the pavement on the road because she tripped on a small pothole, falling hard on her knee. That's when I remembered her for something other than The Kiss back in Melbourne.

"You all right, Whoops?" I said, extending my hand to her at the spot on the curb where she'd stumbled. Last time I met her in Melbourne, we'd gone running at the oval in my neighborhood, and she tripped there, too. She told me then her nickname back home was "Whoops" because of her klutziness and some business about her middle name being "Whoopi" after Whoopi Goldberg. She'd sworn me to secrecy over this information. Who could blame her?

So she did have some smiles under all that sulk. Her green lips turned up, blending into the red blush hot on her face. "Oh, I thought I had finally lived down that name!" She didn't reach for my hand. "I need a minute to rest if you don't mind. That fall really hurt my knee." That's when I figured out maybe she wasn't such a punk girl after all. I sat down on the curb next to her and watched while she licked her middle and index fingers to rub away the blood caked on the scratches on her bare knee. Any true punk girl would leave the bloody scratches on her bruised knee like a badge.

I decided to test my theory. "What bands do you like?" I asked her.

"I don't know." She shrugged. "Which ones do you like?"

"I reckon my favorite punk band right now would be Muleburger."

Pretty quick made-up band name for a daft footy boy, hey? Before her fall, I had been thinking how any of these houses on this street could have a famous person living in them, and I could be walking right by one and not know it. That got me thinking about Eddie Murphy and his character in my favorite movie, *Shrek*. Donkey→Mule. And the uphill walking had been making my stomach grumble harder from hunger. Mmmm→burger.

"Muleburger!" not-punk girl Annabel said. "I love them! They're my favorite."

Yeah, right.

She lost some points for whatever fake persona she'd adopted for the day there, but her cool points shot right back up when we got to her house. Because only Maurice Jackson, my favorite comedian in the world, answered the door! Not only that, but Maurice Jackson happens to be the one actor Miss Shouty and I both like. He's the only interest Miss Shouty and I have in common besides our shared fanaticism for our mutually favorite footy team, the Carlton Blues. But— tragedy!—Miss Shouty was not present to share the most exciting part of our vacation so far!

I never imagined that a day that had started out so pathetic with Miss Shouty and her bloody star maps could wind down with THE Maurice Jackson greeting me at the summer home of the Not-Punk Girl I

Kissed Once. Better yet, his hairy hand held a set of chopsticks with a great-looking maki roll between them, and I could see a chocolate cake sitting on the dining room table in the distance behind him.

At last, Ben's loser vacation had hit a scoring mark, all thanks to the strange girl, Annabel!

Chapter 13

WHEATIES

Machiavelli: "People are by nature changeable. It is easy to persuade them about some particular matter, but it is hard to hold them to that persuasion. Hence it is necessary to provide that when they no longer believe, they can be forced to believe."

Usually when jock guys my age force me to believe something—like what jerks they are—it's by a flick on my head or a light shove against my back when I'm in their way as they breeze past my locker. Yet, I am by my nature changeable, and I have been persuaded that not only has the Ben guy turned out to not be a stupid jock bully, he's also a great guy.

Machiavelli offers no comfort to a prince struck by conscience. I hate that.

I was prepared to despise Ben, but I hadn't been expecting to meet him so soon. The day started out with Tia and Mom having a fight in their bedroom. Mom must have lost because after the fight ended, she came into my room for a grand pronouncement: Even though she should be in the office using her Saturday to organize her files, instead she would stay home so we could have a family day. Because I'm that lucky. Mom's idea of a family day was us going for a run at the UCLA stadium (meaning she jogged while I read a comic book in the stands), then walking around the campus so she could show me the medical school and the law school. She's obviously never heard of the great family day invention called You Bake Some Cookies in the Kitchen While I Play Xbox in My Room. Worse, Tia deserted me to go to her volunteer job, so I was stuck with a whole day alone with Mom.

Mom didn't say it was the reason, but the further fallout of her fight with Tia (that Tia obviously won) was that Mom announced she would soon be taking a few days off work so we could have a family vacation on Catalina. Mom said I could invite Annabel if I wanted. I said I wanted to invite Lucy, too. She said, Who's Lucy?

Hopeless.

I had nothing left to say to her. But I was thinking, *If Annabel and Lucy come along, will they notice you have alien-mother skills, or will you be able to pull off being a regular mom who makes sure we eat balanced meals and keep our jackets zipped up when it's windy, like Angelina and Penny do?*

I saved my conversation energy for Angelina. In the afternoon I called my stepmom to ask how my baby sister Ariel was doing. Angelina knew without being told that I needed to be saved, so she asked me to put Mom on the phone and invited me to spend the night at her place. I knew the air mattress I lugged in my suitcase all the way from NYC would come in handy.

I appreciated Angelina engineering my escape from Westwood but then felt I'd been brought over on false pretenses when I learned I wasn't the only boy whose presence she'd arranged for the evening. Hyped in chocolate-cake chatter mode when I arrived, Angelina blurted out that she'd arranged Ben's coming to her house as a peace offering to Annabel for siding with Annabel's dad in some argument that morning; also, Angelina was *dying* to meet Ben live and in the flesh after all she'd heard of him, and she had a great Aussie celebrity hanging at her house to use as bait! That Maurice guy no one seems to be able to get rid of was hanging out again, and he'd brought along a pile of movie scripts he wanted Angelina to study with him.

If I were my stepsister Annabel, I might have shrieked, "Like, omigod, could I *be* more irritated?"

I'd barely sat down in the living room when Angelina saw Annabel approaching from the window. "Oh! He's cuter than I imagined! If I were a teenager, I'd keep a treasure chest filled with photos of him, too.

But *what* is Annabel wearing? Has she lost her mind? Maurice, quick! To the door to greet them!" Angelina rushed to sit next to me, like she wanted to be all casual and composed when HE walked through her door.

HE, sadly, was as good-looking as his myth had promised, at least if you think that the muscular Calvin Klein underwear model look with a crooked nose is attractive like Annabel does. HE had loose brown hair hanging wild around his face, with an expression as if indifferent to how girls love that broody, hair boy thing, and short brown sideburns growing from his temples. Show-off. At least HE had the dignity to also be somewhat gawky—he hunched his shoulders and let his head hang down, as if embarrassed by his height and muscular appeal. Angelina introduced us all, but HE ignored me, as I had expected. HE followed the Maurice guy into the kitchen like Maurice was the rock star, not Ben. His groupie, Annabel (What was she wearing anyway? Has she lost her mind?), excused herself to the bathroom, hopefully to wash off her ridiculous face. I burned with rage on the couch while Ben howled with laughter at whatever Maurice said to him in the kitchen.

Ben fed my fury further when he soon reappeared in the living room and plopped down next to me on the couch, a plate on his lap. Through bites of sushi he wolfed down most impressively, Ben talked to me like we were old pals instead of new acquaintances and presumed sworn enemies.

"Wheaties—is it all right if I call you that or do you prefer 'Al'?" Can you believe that's Maurice Jackson in the kitchen with Annabel's mum? I can't believe I just met an actual celebrity in LA!"

I pointed out, "Maurice is not famous here."

"Well, he's famous in Australia, but not, like, super Russell Crowe famous—he probably has more of a cult following. My friends and I practically worship him, we know all his acts by heart! Do you know if there's a computer here? I need to e-mail my mates at home and tell them about this!"

My Teenage Mutant Ninja Turtles backpack contained a most impressive laptop, matter of fact. At last, an opportunity for Wheaties to be envied—surely my astounding technology muscle would stand out in superior contrast to Ben's astounding biceps that I wouldn't have figured to be humanly possible on a fifteen-year-old boy unless he trains at the gym with religious fervor. I mumbled, "I brought over my laptop if you want to use it."

"Thanks, mate!" He slapped me on the back, but not in the hostile mean way.

I could feel my rage dissipating like Dad's bank account after he bought our new apartment. I suspected Ben was the type of guy who knew how to judge many of the key mysteries of the dude universe, and I wanted to cross-examine him with

questions: *What is the secret of your success with girls?
What do you bench press, like a million pounds? Do you
know if Lucy likes me and could you possibly ugly yourself up when she's around because I know you're not her
type, but still . . . ?* If I invited HIM to Catalina, imagine all the important guy knowledge I could get out
of him.

The best I could stammer was idle conversation.
"So, how are you liking California so far?"

Maybe it's an Aussie quality of being naturally
friendly, like Lucy, but HE told me, "Listen, I'm
telling you this because I've got to tell someone or I'll
burst. We didn't arrive just yesterday from Australia.
We've been in California a week already, but Dad's
stupid girlfriend made us keep quiet about that. The
vacation so far has been dreadful. I hate this place.
Meeting Maurice Jackson just now—and you too,
mate, hey—is the first good thing that's happened
since coming to this country."

I never thought it possible to meet a person and
think of them as an automatic friend, without waiting
for them to pass certain unspoken tests before you
could confide in them. I asked him, "Is Maurice really
so famous in Australia?"

Maurice makes Angelina laugh too much, which
I'm not sure I like, but nothing else about him particularly recommends him as a brilliant comedian or
actor. The guy is SO depressed. When Angelina reads
lines with him and compliments his delivery,

Maurice shakes his head and goes, "No, I was awful." When Jack announces the network has great confidence that Maurice is going to be one of their biggest stars, Maurice says, "They're bloody idiots." At least Maurice is no dummy. I'm fairly sure Maurice may be right about those network executives' opinion of his talent.

"He's brilliant!" Ben said. Ben had salmon stuck between his gleaming boy-band teeth, but I didn't bother to notify him, not when Annabel returned to the room with her face washed so you could actually see it, and she'd changed from that weird faux-punk-girl costume into normal-girl jammies. Aliens must have abducted my stepsister and replaced her with a robot! What happened to make her de-fashionista for the night, *twice*? Could Ben be so godlike that he inspired Annabel to chill out in the fashion sweepstakes?

As Annabel rocked in the recliner chair opposite us, because she's like her mother and can never sit still, I wondered if Annabel would be embarrassed to know she looked dumbfounded by Ben, when normally she would appear appalled by the pink-salmon tooth gap visible in his mouth. Ben told us, "Maurice was on this sketch comedy show back in Australia for a couple years. He had this hilarious postman character who attacked dog owners as if he was the attack dog himself. When characters getting their mail would be all, 'How's your day, postman?' he would be all, 'Ruff ruff grrrrrrrrrrrrrr,' cuz you know he does look rather like a mangy dog."

Ben had gotten up from the couch to act out Maurice's postman dog routine, but when he finished, Annabel and I sat quiet, thinking there was more to the routine—or maybe something was lost in translation? Ben sat back down. "Trust me, it was really funny," he said. He scarfed down what had to be his seventh maki roll before diving right into a bite of chocolate cake. His six-pack of abs must contain six stomachs of food-storage space underneath.

The TV played in the background, with a familiar feminine voice suddenly announcing, *Feel your freshest self!* For the first time since I've known her—and I've known her since nursery school—Annabel's body froze in her seat. Her eyes widened and moved to meet mine, then at Ben, then back at me again. I lunged for the remote and clicked off the TV super fast, like I was a gunslinger from the Old West. Annabel's body unfroze itself.

"Where's Lucy?" I asked Annabel, but my ungrateful stepsister ignored me, distracted by her mother's squeal of laughter at something Maurice said or did in the kitchen. Annabel jumped up from her seat to police the situation in there.

Ben leaned in to me. He muttered, "Lucy stayed home. Something about feminine troubles."

"Oh, man," I said. "Don't want to hear any more."

"Exactly," Ben stated, and suddenly I knew, in that

psychic way I have, like how I know that Tia and Mom will choose an Angelina Jolie movie at the video rental store over a decent disaster flick: Ben and I were going to be friends, not enemies. So much for Signor Machiavelli.

Chapter 14

Annabel

I caught Ben checking out my bare legs when I wore the short black skirt, but I'm unclear whether he found my Annoy-Jack fashion statement attractive or not. All this worry about looks and wondering about Ben is exhausting, to be honest. I'm not sure I can sustain all the mental energy that goes into it.

I wouldn't mind a satellite link directly to Ben's brain that could provide a feed report telling me exactly what Ben thinks of me. That would make our short time together much easier. Sample report readings from Ben's brain could be like: outfit—very hot; streaky hair—moderately hot; Whoops falling down in front of her crush—completely NOT hot, you idiot!

OWWWWWWWWWW, I hurt my knee REALLY bad! After my fall, part of me wanted to play damsel-in-distress and hold on to Ben's arm as I hobbled back up the street alongside him, the way I did last time I fell in front of him, back in Melbourne. The other part of me, the matured part who so admired his footy muscles (from a purely scientific standpoint, of course—I appreciated the discipline that goes into making those muscles, rather than just shallow appreciation of that WOW bod), that part wanted Ben to think of me as being strong like him. Okay, mostly I wanted to bolt home, change out of the stupid heavy leather jacket and boots and tight skirt, which were probably the reason for me losing my balance and falling anyway, clean and bandage the knee wound, then take an aspirin and call it a night.

I longed for a private moment to conclude my humiliation, to hang my head in shame and reacquaint myself with that *om* thing, but Mom had to invite all these people to the house. If I had a bigger allowance, I would buy her a self-help book not just on how to find and keep love, but on learning to tone down her overly social tendencies. Like I didn't know she worked the whole Ben-Maurice situation just so she could get a look at my crush! I mean, thanks, but—back off! Now Jack is ticked off with me *and* Angelina!

If Jack didn't like my punk-girl outfit, he hadn't said so—which I thought rather rude. Why did I bother with all that effort if I couldn't even get a rise out of him? I think he was about to react angrily when he first saw me, but then Penny did that weird wife-telepathy thing with Jack where she shook her head at him and pressed the palms of her hands down as if to say, "Keep your cool." The best I got out of him was seeing him take an *om* deep breath before telling me, "I like your new look, Annabel. Are you trying out for clown school?"

So. Ignorant. No wonder Maurice is Dad's biggest comedian client—they share being completely unfunny in common.

Back home at the house up the hill, I dodged into the bathroom to clean the knee wound and wash the rebel-girl colors from my face. BLECH! I didn't feel like washing my hair to get out the ugly streaks so I tied my hair back into a loose knot, and changed into flannel pajama bottoms and a loose NY Mets T-shirt. I like Ben MORE THAN EVER now that I've seen him again, but really, I was tired from all the work that had gone into my looks for the day. I must be spending too much time with Lucy, because I kept hearing her Aussie voice in my head, chiding me, *If a boy only cares about the way you look, he's not worth knowing, hey Annabel?* I needed to let my stomach stick out and wear comfy slippers on my feet whether Ben thought that was hot or not.

When I went into the kitchen to see why my mother was embarrassing me with her loud laughter, she handed me a piece of cake, which I knew to be an incentive of some sort. I took the plate and waited to hear her latest scheme. Sure enough: "I think we should have a slumber party tonight!" Angelina said. "Al brought his air mattress over, we've got a sleeping bag for Ben, Maurice can sleep on the couch, and we'll call Lucy to join us and she can share your room. We'll play Pictionary and watch some movies! Ariel's been sleeping through the night, so c'mon, it'll be fun!"

Maurice mimed a charade behind her, one hand on his heart, the other on his forehead, while his foot kicked a pretend ball. I believe he was mocking my Ben crush.

"Hah hah," I stated, not laughing. The guy is so not funny—I don't get the big deal over him. The only evidence in Maurice's favor right now is Ben's enthusiasm for him.

I was about to say NO WAY to Angelina's terrible plan. Her spontaneous calls for slumber parties were fun back in Manhattan when my girlfriends from school hung out, even though our noise drove Harvey nuts. But in this parallel LA universe of steps and crushes and confusion and me with the messy hair and lazy outfit, Angelina's idea for a slumber party with four teens and two very old people, all of mixed genders, was BAD BAD BAD. All the LA smog must have infiltrated Angelina's grasp on sanity.

But Ben had joined us in the kitchen and heard her. He said, "REALLY? That would be graayate! Dad and his girlfriend wouldn't mind some time to themselves, I'm sure."

"Ben! You are just TOO thoughtful!" Angelina squealed. I looked around the kitchen for a paper bag to place over my head. She turned to Maurice and said, like Ben wasn't even standing right there, "I love this boy!" Before I could protest this horrible further humiliation, Angelina's plan steamrolled out of my control.

The "fast-talking phone lady," as my friends from home call my mother because of all the telephone-product commercials she's been in, had picked up the phone and hit the speed dial faster than Wheaties had clicked off that *Feel your freshest self* commercial a few minutes ago. Angelina said, "Hi, Jack, it's me . . . oh, get over it . . . can you put Ben's dad on the phone . . . because we'd like to invite Ben to stay over tonight—you know, give his dad and the girlfriend some time alone . . . yes, Wheaties is here . . . of course the boys would sleep in the living room . . . well, Ben doesn't look jet-lagged to me . . . I agree, we'd love Lucy to come over and share Annabel's room tonight . . . so what do you care if Maurice is here . . . didn't the network notes suggest he should spend more time with real teenagers to help loosen him up in the family scenes . . . hello, overbearing one—slumber party with real live opportunity for Maurice to interact with four actual teens!"

Angelina rolled her eyes. She placed one hand over the mouthpiece and shooed us away with her other hand. I could hear Jack shouting something through the phone, but Angelina ignored him, unconcerned, and whispered at us, "Go on, you guys! I'll get Jack to bring over some pajamas and a spare toothbrush for Ben when he drops off Lucy. Annabel, should I ask Lucy to bring any DVDs from their collection down the road? Oh, never mind—go ask Al what movie we should rent; he's the expert."

I believe it's safe to say Jack and Angelina's truce may officially be over. I hope Penny doesn't need any more driving lessons.

Maurice's and my "truce" (if you can call him always hanging around and me pretending he's not there a "truce") needed to be figured out before this slumber party could get started. I tugged on Maurice's arm and dragged him outside the house for a private moment. There was no time to be subtle, so I just came out with it. I said, "I think it's time you tell me your intentions with my mom, comedy boy."

He dared to laugh at me instead of being insulted by my sarcasm! Then he sat down on the porch stairs and gestured for me to sit alongside him. I didn't. I stood at ground level hoping to stare him down and not smile on the off chance he did or said something funny.

Maurice said, "Comedy boy doesn't know many people here in LA, and he would very much like to get to know your mother better. But he's aware of her situation, and assures you he won't be making any dishonorable moves on a married lady." He did this exaggerated bow down to me like he was a butler or a doorman.

"Good," I said. I started to go back up the porch stairs, but he stretched his long body out sideways along the stairs and put his legs up against the porch rail to block my way.

"Not so fast," he said. "Now there's something I'm going to tell you. You don't seem to notice, and her husband back in New York doesn't notice enough, and your own father is in no position to appreciate her, but I think your mother is fantastic. She is kind and funny and warm and . . ."

"She's also beautiful," I pointed out. Because I didn't want Maurice to think I didn't know what he probably really notices most about her.

"Is she?" He made a face like he was trying to imagine what she looked like and ponder that image. "Yes, I suppose she is. But this town is full of beautiful women. Few of them have the heart your mother does."

"I don't get it. Are you trying to be funny?"

"There's nothing funny about this situation."

"So you do get it," I said. "Mom is off-limits."

"I get it," he said. "But she can still be my friend, right? Cut an Aussie a break, will ya?"

"She can be your friend," I told Maurice. "Just nothing more. Promise me."

Maurice said, "How very generous of you. Shall we have official papers drawn up? No more sulking faces from the daughter in exchange for a binding, legal agreement that the dreaded comedy boy shall not act with dishonor upon Lady Angelina?" He stood up and reached his hands to the sky and dramatically cried out, "Was it Hamlet who said . . ."

And I told him, "You're still not funny, Maurice. But you've got a deal."

Chapter 15

Lucy

When Mum and Dad bought bunk beds for my bedroom, they expected Annabel and I would be sharing my room when she visited from New York. I doubt they anticipated when they moved from Australia that Angelina might also come with the Annabel-in-LA-with-us package, and I'm sure they never expected it would be me sharing the bedroom with Annabel at Angelina's temporary quarters instead of Annabel bunking at our house. Annabel's room here has a trundle bed like her room in New York, so, like old times when she visited us in Sydney or I visited her in Manhattan, we're rooming together again—she on one bed level and me a short distance away. We can be exhausted beyond belief from the day's adventures yet can't resist talking in the dark through the late night. It's our habit.

"Do you like Wheaties?" she whispered to me. The clock light read 1:50 A.M. I thought she'd fallen asleep because we hadn't spoken since 1:43 A.M.

I knew my answer wasn't the one she wanted to hear, but I had to call it straight. "I like him a lot," I whispered back. "Just not like-like."

"Oh, poor Wheaties. Crushed by his crush. Sometimes dags just can't catch a break."

Here's the other thing that annoys me besides the big idea that everyone should be coupled up—that if a guy who's basically a good fellow likes a girl, and she doesn't like him back in the same way, then somehow it's the girl who's supposed to feel bad, as if she did something wrong by simply not sharing his attraction. Wheaties of all people should know about chemistry: Either you have it or you don't. We don't. One-sided chemistry doesn't count. I wish I didn't feel like me wanting to only be his friend could stop us from being friends altogether. Wheaties is definitely acting like he'd like to move our friendship into new territory, and I dread the moment I have to put the Stop sign up in his face. I don't know what I'm supposed to say that won't be mean but at the same time lets him know: LUCY—NOT INTERESTED! Is there a rule book for this stuff?

Also, maybe Wheaties and I aren't related by blood, but the connection is still too close for me. Umm— gross! Ben and Annabel are connected in the same step-to-step way, but in my mind, Mum and Ben's dad were never truly married to each other in their hearts, and our two families hardly blended long enough to qualify us as one real family, the way Wheaties and Annabel are. Even though Ben and Annabel are a teensy bit connected through Mum's brief union to Ben's dad, Ben and Annabel together wouldn't qualify as being . . . well, as being insects having a party, as Angus would say.

I told Annabel, "Wheaties the dag already caught a break. Like, he practically broke my foot when we did the psycho salsa dance." If I wasn't so sleepy, I might get out of bed for an ice pack to place on the $%&! bruise Wheaties accidentally gave me when he stepped too hard on my foot while trying to mimic the dance Angelina had taught us.

After the Pictionary game and the ritual viewing of Angelina and Maurice's favorite '80s movie, *Ferris Bueller's Day Off,* and the ritual making of her favorite treat, s'mores (that lady really knows how to throw a slumber party!), Angelina mentioned something about starting to miss New York, something about the energy and buzz you can only experience there. Annabel, who had relaxed into a good mood by then from the funny movie, yummy treats, and the Ben nearness, didn't miss her opportunity to remind Angelina about one of their favorite things to do in Manhattan besides shopping and going to Broadway shows. They both love to watch the underground performers in the Times Square subway station. A and A love the break-dancers and the calypso bands, but their favorite act is a guy they call the "psycho salsa dancer" because he's a short Latin dancer-man who wears a bolero jacket and performs amazing, passionate salsa dances with a lovely female—who turns out to be a mannequin. He's so good that, according to A-Squared, his mannequin appears to come alive—spectators have to look carefully before realizing he's not dancing with a real person.

Of course, Maurice demanded Angelina show him the dance. She stepped into his arms and went limp against him while he led her through an atrocious set of dance missteps that looked more like a bad game of Twister with a dead person than like a mock salsa dance. Their version of the psycho dance had me, Ben, and Wheaties howling with laughter on the couch, and even Annabel couldn't help but giggle. Somehow I cannot picture Harvey ever trying to lead Angelina through a psycho salsa dance—or even wanting to. Our group laughed so hard we woke up the baby, so while Angelina went to comfort her, Ben and Wheaties decided they needed to try this dance too. I thought only extreme torture could make boys want to dance, but I reckoned if Maurice wanted to do it, then it was cool by them. Only because I love Annabel so much did I not jump right into Ben's space to be his partner—that's how much I wanted to avoid contact with Wheaties. I did want to try that dance, though, but not with sweaty Maurice. Annabel clearly couldn't get enough of playing the mannequin psycho-dancing in Ben's arms, so I took Wheaties' hand to join in the dance tryout.

Let's just say Wheaties pressed a little too hard into me and I felt more of him than I cared to and leave it at that.

I whispered to Annabel, "Wheaties is a dag that needs some dance lessons before taking on another dance partner of the female kind." This slumber party was fun, but I am dreading the next round of all this step-togetherness. Tia and Wheaties' mum are taking us on a camping adventure to Catalina Island, and Wheaties had better not think the cozy campfire atmosphere is the place for him to try another move on me, because one more stray of his hand somewhere on my person and no more Saint Lucy. I am going to have to tell that little fellow off.

Annabel murmured, "Aww, he tried. Not every boy can be as well-coordinated and perfect as Bennnnnnnnnnnnn." For a girl I found deep in sulk when I arrived this evening, embarrassed by her mum's slumber party idea and in an uneasy peace with Maurice, she'd sure enjoyed herself watching Ben have such a good time.

"Do you think you will kiss Ben again?" I asked.

"I hope so! Maybe Catalina will be the place! Did you hear Wheaties invite him?" She went silent again, then: "Lucy?"

"Yeah?"

"Have you ever kissed a boy?"

"Kind of."

Without warning, she turned on the nightstand lamp. After I opened my eyes from the squint of the sudden light, I saw Annabel on the bed above my trundle. She lay on her side, her head on her hand, the silly orange and black streaks still visible in her unusually unmannered hair. "Who! When! Why didn't you tell me before now!" She no longer bothered to whisper.

"Turn the light out! I'm sleepy." I turned over away from her and pulled the blanket over my head to block out the lamp light.

She kicked my leg. "C'mon, Luce! Spill!"

I turned back over to face her again. "Will you turn out the light if I do? My eyes are tired." She turned the lamp off. The darkness encouraged my secret to spill from my lips. "Remember when I went to that theater camp in Sydney for a few weeks last summer—well, winter here?"

"Yeah. You were graaayate as Annie in *Annie Get Your Gun*. Dad sent me a copy of the video. Hey, wait a minute, let me guess who it was! I can't believe you didn't tell me this before now."

"You never asked before."

"That's because I assume you're going to tell me if something major like that happens! Lucy!" I felt a kick on my leg again, but this time the rub was more like a tickle. Annabel said, "Wait, don't tell me, I'm gonna guess who the boy was. Wait . . . I know! The cowboy actor kid who sang 'Girl That I Marry'? Nice-looking boy but kinda over-the-top theatrical, like one of those bad child actors on TV who are all fake and 'Oh, *yes*, Father, that would be *won*-der-ful!'"

"How did you know! Yes, that boy!" Robbie from theater camp was a lovely boy but WAYYYYY too into musical theater. At age fourteen, he'd already been in eight theater-camp shows since kindie, and several professional dinner theater ones as well. He lived to perform show tunes.

"But didn't you *have* to kiss him for the show?"

"Yes. Annie and the Frank Butler character did have a kissing scene."

"Luce. Lucy, Lucy, Lucy. Lucinda of Naïve-ville. I don't think that counts."

Oh! Miss Experience getting all uppity now with whether *my* experience counted. "Excuse me, but it does count. Not only did I kiss him for the show, but we also kissed on the walk back home after rehearsal. TWICE. Once in the park and once in a booth at McDonald's where we stopped for a Coke."

In her leprechaun-lilt voice she uses to tease about my undying love of Lucky Charms cereal, Annabel sang out this ditty: "Lovely Lucinda, from Naïve-ville straight to The Land of the Fallen Woman ye are . . ." It was a good thing the boys were in the living room; sometimes no one besides me and Annabel understand the way we talk to one another.

I laughed. "Shut up."

She laughed too, but still wanted to know: "So how was it? The kissing? The TWICE?"

"It was okay," I whispered. "Nice."

Even with the darkness where truths seem to blurt out easier, I had lied to her—don't know why. Either I was too shy or Robbie had rubber lips, because each kiss we shared was sloppy and awkward. His hands didn't even touch me, and he was stiff and nervous as he leaned over to touch his mouth on mine. And once he'd done it, that was it, no more interest. The whole thing felt more like a science experiment than a romantic one—like while we were doing it, he was thinking kissing a girl was totally overrated, and I was thinking, why did I choose you to experience this with when I could have saved myself for Orlando Bloom?

I didn't care to discuss the disappointing kissing thing any longer. I whispered to Annabel, "How come you never stay over at our house?" I've been wondering about this a lot, but sometimes it's easier to ask certain questions in the dark.

She waited a while before answering, and when she spoke, it was slowly, like she was figuring it out as she went along. "Part of it has to do with Mom. Angelina and I gripe at each other a lot, but I guess I am kind of worried about her too. I don't want her to feel alone in this strange place. She's been very sad even though she always acts like everything is good. And the other part is . . . well, when I used to visit you all in Sydney, it was great, but it was like playing pretend family, Oz style. But now that you're here, it's more real—like Jack all of a sudden telling me what I can and can't wear. And trying to figure out your family rhythm and where I fit into that. It's not that I don't feel welcome or like part of your family, it's just . . . more confusing now. I can't explain."

"But you know we'd love if you stayed with us more, right? Maybe if you stayed with us more, it would feel less confusing. Me and Angus . . ."

". . . and Josephine Snickercross?" Annabel interrupted.

"Who?" I said, even though I wasn't being totally honest with her again. I didn't know Annabel even knew about Josephine. "I don't know what you're talking about."

"That's exactly what I'm talking about," Annabel whispered.

The clock read 2:15 A.M. We didn't talk anymore after that.

Chapter 16

Ben

During the miserable week we secretly traveled around Northern California, land of stupid, quaint San Francisco with all the queues and the fog-rimmed, cliff-side coastline that made me carsick, many times after the natives heard our foreign accents, they would ask how we were enjoying our trip. It was like they couldn't wait for us to congratulate them on what a supposedly great place they lived in. After being reassured by Dad and Miss Shouty that, yes, Dad and Miss S left their hearts in bloody San Francisco and that, of course, Gilroy, the garlic capital of the world, was the nicest-smelling town they'd ever been to, and sure indeedy, the outlet mall there rocked, then the natives would want to know: "Where else are you visiting besides Northern California?" When Miss Shouty shouted at them,

"DISNEYLAND AND LOS ANGELES," inevitably the Northern California people would roll their eyes and sigh. Sometimes they'd even pat our backs like to comfort us, which made sense after the Monterey tour guide told us Northern California people look down their noses at Southern California for being a vast wasteland of shopping malls and smog.

So maybe Southern California is smoggy and you have to drive long distances in lots of traffic to get anywhere, but so what. IT'S SO MUCH BETTER DOWN HERE!

If I was a science guy like Wheaties with the ginger hair covering up that small head with the big brain, I could probably make a statistical chart to determine whether my newfound love for Los Angeles was because with all the step-people around, I haven't been trapped with Miss Shouty all the time, or whether it has anything to do with The Not-Punk Girl I'm Thinking About Kissing Again. I don't know about statistics, but I do know how to do a play-by-play account of the important events that have made LA my favorite place in America so far.

- ✓ Our first night at Annabel and her fun mum's house: fantastic sleepover. GOT TO MEET MAURICE JACKSON! S'mores and psycho salsa dancing—best inventions ever? In the morning, Dad came to pick me up along with Miss Shouty, who promptly SCREAMED with excitement in Maurice's presence. While she was in the loo, I heard Maurice phone Jack and ask him to please give proper warning whenever Miss Shouty will be present so Maurice can know the places to avoid. Maurice elevated from favorite comedian to godlike figure in my eyes.

✓ Day after sleepover: Free at last, hallelujah, free at last! Me, Lucy, Annabel, and Wheaties got sprung from the adults and dropped off on our own at a fantastic outdoor shopping arcade called The Grove. Never cared for shopping before but didn't mind checking out the Hawk Skate, Quicksilver, and Nike stores. Decided only in America would it be possible for a skater-god like Tony Hawk to get his own store. Approve. Rode the old-fashioned trolley car around the mall, then watched boring Hollywood summer-bonanza movie in the big cinema with plush chairs and monster-size popcorn. Threw popcorn at Annabel sitting next to me. Shared her Coke. During the distracting loud parts of the movie, allowed my hand to accidentally on purpose graze her knee. More importantly, while Annabel and Lucy were in the bathroom, learned from Wheaties about some guy called Machiavelli whose teachings I plan to apply on the footy oval when I get home to Melbourne. Can you say "ruthless?"

✓ Next day: The moms took us on a picnic at Griffith Park. Walked around Observatory alone with Annabel. Resisted urge to take her hand. Didn't resist when she took mine. Pondered why I started to like her anyway since I barely remembered her when I got here, and now find myself equally confused as to why I am attracted by her ever-changing looks and moods. What would Machiavelli say about this? He'd probably advise something like: It's okay to mess around with her as you will soon be going home to Melbourne, but she's not the type of girl who would be satisfied to just experiment in the lip-locking sport—she'd probably demand to be elevated from kissing partner to full-on girlfriend, and look how that's turned out for Dad—so don't be in such a rush, boy-o.

✓ Later that day: strolled along the Hollywood Walk of Fame. Annabel stuck her hands in Claudette Colbert's imprint even though we had no idea who she is; we just liked the sound of her name. Lucy went for Audrey Hepburn's hands, while Wheaties chose Johnny Cash's. I kept my hands to myself, Mr. Machiavelli, you bet I did. Saw Miss Shouty place her hands in Marilyn Monroe's while Dad snapped her photo and was reminded that getting involved with blondes might not be all it's cracked up to be if the blondes are crack-ups themselves.

✓ Next day: The dads (well, my dad, Jack, and Tia) took the lads (me, Angus, and Wheaties) to Dodger Stadium. Got to see first live American baseball game! Learned philosophical aspects of

"The Show" from Wheaties. Learned to hate all things Yankee from Wheaties and Jack. Learned Angus's favorite team is the Seattle Mariners, for reasons having nothing to do with baseball.

✓ Night after Dodgers game: BEST DINNER EVER IN THE HISTORY OF MY LIFE! Went to a street hot-dog stand called Pink's Famous Chili Dogs. First celebrity sighting of star not just famous in Australia: Wheaties claims we stood in line behind Pauly Shore, who starred in some "cable classic" movie Wheaties loves called *Son-in-Law*. Annabel assured me I should not be impressed. Still am. Shared outside table with Annabel, Lucy, and Wheaties while the adults sat separately from us, bless them. As the four of us kids made our own musical symphony of belches and croaking noises, decided we could form our own musical group, like a vicious thrasher-band version of *The Brady Bunch*. Since there are four of us and we're quasi-related, we could call ourselves The Quads. Or not. Developing musical talent would get in way of footy practice. Plus rehearsals would be hard, given we live in different quads of the world. Resolve to think of we four non-step steps as The Quads anyway, as their collective parts of the whole LA experience have made this vacation tolerable, at last.

Surprisingly, the best part of our trip had nothing to do with a famous place or a great chili dog or the pretty girl I've been thinking about too much. We still had several days left in LA until we returned home to Melbourne when—thank *you*, Reserve Bank of Australia—our Australian currency got devalued! Wheaties explained to me what this meant for the rest of our vacation in America: Basically, each American dollar Dad had in his wallet that had just been exchanged from Australian money on the day of the devaluation was now worth more like seventy cents for Dad. So if Dad had x amount of money budgeted for our hotel, car, and entertainment, now he had about 30 percent less of x. Lousy for Dad, yeah, and I didn't much appreciate having less spending money, either, but I may write a letter of thanks to the economists in Canberra who made that devaluation decision.

With Dad near broke and unable to change our air tickets so we could go home earlier, he reluctantly accepted Jack and Penny's offer for us to spend the remainder of our trip at their place. The savings on the accommodation costs allowed him to hold on to the rental car for the duration of our trip and still afford food and entertainment costs. Lucy temporarily moved up the street to share Annabel's room, Dad and Miss Shouty took over the bunk beds in her room, and I got the living room sofa near the ace satellite TV with the many ESPN and cartoon channels. Ben is loving America now, baby—and especially loving no longer sharing a hotel suite with Her Loudness.

Lucy and Annabel and their families are so lucky.

There are always lots of people around, places to see, things to do—they're always go-go-go. It's like this mix-and-match: You two go here with Penny and Angelina, you three with the dads, you four on your own. By the time Dad, Miss Shouty, and I moved over to Jack and Penny's to stay, I was ready to enshrine Penny, our self-appointed concierge, for arranging all the fun activities for us. But Penny said I had it wrong. She said, "No, it's me who should be thanking all of you who are here from New York and Australia. I've been here half a year myself and haven't seen much till now, so having everyone here is a good opportunity for me to finally explore the city that I reckon it's about time to accept I live in."

I'm still wishing that if I have to have a potential future stepmum, she could be someone like Penny. The only thing different I'd wish for in the lady would be that she's not a secret smoker like Penny. I had the TV on very low late that first night we spent at Jack and Penny's house, so when I heard some shuffling in the kitchen, I got up from the couch to inspect. Maurice the God says Los Angeles is a city built on violence and greed, so I figured I'd better make sure a burglar hadn't entered my new favorite sanctuary. I found no intruder in the kitchen but saw that the sliding doors to the patio deck had been left open. When I went outside, ready to tackle the intruder, I saw Penny sitting at the patio umbrella table, puffing on a smoke.

"You startled me!" she whispered. The nighttime

air was chilly so I placed the blanket I had carried from the couch (in case I needed to smother a burglar) around Penny's shoulders. "Aren't you sweet?" she murmured.

I sat down next to her. "Just don't let on to Dad's girlfriend. She thinks I'm a nightmare."

"She doesn't think that." Penny took a long drag on her cigarette, then exhaled. "She thinks you don't like her."

With Penny I can be honest. "Well then, that's one thing she's right about." I considered taking the cigarette from Penny's fingers and stubbing it out, along with reciting some vital information about how smoking will severely mess with her cardiovascular workouts, but I didn't. Penny saw me eyeing her cigarette and said, "So I sneak an occasional smoke late at night when I can't sleep. It's my private little indulgence, even if Lucy is on to me, and I don't want to hear a lecture from you."

I shrugged. "I wasn't going to give you one."

"Yes, you were."

"Okay, I was." Penny knows me. Miss Shouty would never figure out what I was going to do like that.

Penny said, "You should give her a chance. So she's a little loud and rough round the edges. But she loves your dad and will take good care of him. It might seem far away now, but you won't be living at home that many more years. Who's going to care for your old man then, hey? Doesn't he deserve a mate, mate?"

"I liked it better when you were with him."

"Ben, you and I both know your dad and I made a big mistake getting married when we did. We were both too messed up with grief then to understand the connection we'd made. And may I remind you? You didn't care much for me either when Patrick and I first got together."

"That's not true!"

Penny laughed and took another drag. "It is true! The first time I met you, Lucy and Angus were with their gran, so your dad took you and me to dinner for us to have a proper meet, and you didn't speak ONE word to me the whole dinner. But you made sure to slurp your spaghetti extra long and dramatically, so I'd know you were at least capable of making sound. You were dreadful! And have you forgotten the pet frog you used to somehow conveniently misplace in my handbag? Or the footy game you insisted your dad attend when I was in the hospital getting a cast on my broken arm and could have really used the lift home?"

OUCH! Miss Shouty is the hypochondriac, but perhaps I suffer my own ailment in repressed-memory syndrome, because Penny's recollections were true. How was it that Penny had changed from being a step-mum invasion to being someone I liked?

"But then remember what happened?" Penny said. "You relaxed enough to get used to me. And once you'd gotten used to me, you were able to get to know me and discover, oh, shocker, Penny's not actually a stepmonster!"

"I'm sorry if I made you miserable." Tia tells Wheaties he's a "late bloomer," but for all my blooming height and girl experience, maybe it's me who's the late bloomer—about five years late in offering an apology to Penny.

"No worries!" Penny affectionately tapped her foot against mine under the table. "You gave me great practice for when Annabel came into my life. You were nothing compared to her. But now look at Annabel and me—we're okay, right? The girl who could stare daggers into my soul when she first came to Sydney has turned into a lovely stepdaughter, at least on most days. You never know which Annabel mood you're going to meet: happy, mad, giddy, brainy. But I think you've figured that out for yourself by now, hey Ben?" In the moonlight I saw her wink at me.

How come these things are supposed to be private and personal but everyone seems to know there is something brewing between me and Annabel? That's almost reason enough not to pursue it, simply to prove everyone wrong.

Penny stubbed out her cigarette and stood up. She took the blanket from her shoulders and wrapped it back around mine. When I jumped in my seat, it wasn't from her quick pat on my chilly head, but from the howling I heard from the trees behind the patio. "What was that?" I asked Penny.

"Coyote, probably," Penny said.

Coyotes in LA? I asked her, "Do you think there will be coyotes on Catalina?" My last big adventure with The Quads before going back to Australia will be an overnight camping trip on some island about twenty-five miles off the coast of LA. I've been outdoor camping many times, but never near coyotes, I don't think. Yeah, believe it—this hulking footy team captain is scared to death of animals that prey in the dark. I'm not embarrassed to admit it, either. The punk girls in Melbourne LOVE when I confess this secret. Revealing it to them never fails to earn me dozens of kisses, and not just any old lippy action, but the kind with the open mouths.

Penny laughed as I gripped the blanket tight around my shoulders. She said, "I don't know about coyotes on Catalina, but I've heard there are buffalo roaming the middle interior of the island. But Ben, darling, I don't think it's coyotes or buffalo in the night you have to fear there. It's the two fourteen-year-old girls who will keep you up all night, giggling in the tent next to yours!"

Chapter 17

WHEATIES

The first runner-up for the Wheaties' Most Embarrassing Interaction with an Australian So Far This Summer award goes to . . . Ben's dad's girlfriend! Her acceptance speech can acknowledge her outstanding talent for persistent, loud questioning as to whether Tia was my mom's assistant or roommate—she didn't understand why I spent so much time with Tia. Worse, after Ben snapped at her with the explanation, she spent a half hour stuck to my side like she was my Siamese twin when we visited the Hollywood Walk of Fame, droning on with equal, loud persistence about how she loves the music of Melissa Etheridge. Actually, that last part was more embarrassing for her than me.

And, ladies and gentlemen, the grand-slam prize winner for the Wheaties' Most Embarrassing Interaction with an Australian So Far This Summer award goes to . . . drumroll, please . . . Lucy Crosswell!

With my bad luck, someone probably recorded the scene and will get big reality-TV dollars to replay it on the giant screen at Dodger Stadium. Cue corny stadium music, ahhhh, the crowd goes wild in anticipation of watching geeky Wheaties get shot down by the Australian babe.

Scene Setting:

INTERIOR—movie theatre at The Grove. Annabel and Ben sit a few seats away from us, separated from me and Lucy by the mounds of shopping bags Annabel accidentally on purpose has placed on the seats between us.

The Move

During a particularly scary movie moment that has audience members screaming, I decide to go for it. I do the classic yawn-arm maneuver passed down through generations of teen-sex comedy films, where the male yawns and stretches his arm out, landing that arm around the shoulder of the pretty girl sitting next to him.

The Moment of Mortification:

When my arm descends around Lucy's shoulders, the girl I don't think is even paying attention to me because she's so into the movie suddenly turns to me. "NO!" sweet, quiet Lucy yells, louder than the movie explosion, louder even than Ben's dad's girlfriend.

The Further Moment of Mortification:

Lucy grabs my hand from where it lays limp around her shoulder and throws it back over to my lap.

I think the only people in the theater who didn't turn their heads around to gape at us were Ben and Annabel, who were lost in their own private daze.

I guess if I can be grateful for anything, it's that if I am stuck on an overnight camping trip with the girl who brutally shot me down, at least my mom isn't here too. Right now I have only that one scene with Lucy that plays in my head in horrible slo-mo constant repeat. I'm confident that Mom joining with me, Ben, Lucy, and Annabel on the excursion to Catalina Island would have been the exact formula to produce a situation that could top my previously attained most embarrassing moments.

Mom bailed on the trip, of course. The Catalina adventure was Tia's idea for us all to spend quality time together so Mom could get to know my friends (or maybe that was Tia's way for Mom to really get to know me?). Then Mom's biggest corporate client decided they needed to have a hostile takeover of a competing company, like, *now*. Of course they did! Why wouldn't they? I don't know if I was mad at Mom for not coming or mad because that meant Annabel, Lucy, and Ben knew she didn't come because her work was more important.

I was mad, but also a little relieved. I had been dreading Mom doing some hostile takeover on any last remaining appreciation Lucy had for me. I imagined Mom interrogating Lucy around the campfire on Catalina: "What do you mean you're not on the honors track at school, Lucy? Then you need to dump your extracurriculars so you'll have more study time. Surfing club is a waste of time! You love *drama* club? Actors make no money—you know that, right? Join the debate team if you must have one extracurricular activity—at least debate practice might improve your enunciation. Lucy, dear, not everyone here understands what you're saying all the time with that Australian accent of yours. What, you didn't know that? Why are you crying, Lucy? Did someone die?"

For all that I'm relieved not to have big-mouthed Mom here, there's still a huge silence between me and Lucy that no amount of Annabel chattering or sounds of night animals and ocean crashing here on Catalina can drown out. Lucy's the one who rejected me, so I don't get why since then she acts like we're still friends. It's almost like she's trying too hard. At the Hollywood Walk of Fame, Lucy walked blocks out of her way to find my hero Johnny Cash's imprint for me. It was Lucy who suggested Jack take the boys to the Dodgers game because she said the Dodgers used to be from Brooklyn way back when and were dreaded rivals of the Yankees—how did an Australian know that all of a sudden? Lucy's even the gastronomic genius who asked if we could all meet up for dinner that night for hot dogs, because she said now that I'm not a vegan anymore (that only lasted like a few months back in seventh grade), I would love the meat fill-'er-up at Pink's. Everyone thought her choice of dinner place was graayate, but while I enjoyed my chili dog very much, I couldn't help but suspect the Pink's choice was her way of saying that she doesn't like me because I'm too scrawny.

And now I'm trapped on an island with her! *Oy vey.* I'll be glad when this summer vacation ends, once Dad and Angelina have figured out their situations, and we can all go back to our regularly-scheduled lives. So my freshman year at high school will start like all the other school years, with Wheaties the Geek having the brains and not the babe, but at least I'm used to that. Familiarity is comforting. I don't fit in here. Lucy and Ben have their Australian-ness and sportiness in common, Ben and Annabel have their nauseating mutual crush that I wish they'd just act on and get it over with so the rest of us can stop suffering through the flirtation, and Annabel and Lucy are as close as real sisters who have different accents could be. Where's the room for me? The only one of us four that I'm enjoying hanging out with is the one I expected to despise: Ben. He's a great guy, and I could totally be his sidekick except I have too much self-respect to demand anything less than a costarring, equally billed role. And Annabel makes sure no one besides her gets too much of Ben's attention, anyway.

On the boat ride to Catalina, Ben and I sat together, girl-free for once, on the inside deck of the boat while Lucy, Annabel, and Tia stood on the upper deck as the boat sailed out of the harbor at Long Beach. We clocked maybe fifteen minutes without them, having a perfectly fine conversation about my new warrior-philosopher discovery, Sun Tzu, the Chinese war-god who wrote a treatise called *The Art of War*, and about the dread of stepmoms not being worth getting into a Dad-war in my experience, until Annabel had to ruin our dude time. She came down to the lower deck and grabbed Ben's hand, completely ignoring me. "C'mon, Ben, there are some whales swimming alongside the boat, you have to see!" She didn't bother to ask me to come along, but I didn't want to join them anyway. I stayed seated by myself, heeding the advice of Master Tzu: "Be extremely subtle, even to the point of form-lessness. Be extremely mysterious, even to the point of soundlessness. Thereby you can be the director of the opponent's fate."

When the boat docked at Santa Catalina Island, we walked through the town of Avalon, had lunch, explored the Botanical Garden, and then hiked to the Hermit Gulch Campground. I wondered if Hermit Gulch was a real person (maybe with a twin named Kermit) and if he had any warrior philosophies worth investigating, perhaps etched on a campground tree, somewhere that I could escape the group and read all about it.

That evening, we pitched our tents while Tia gathered wood to make us a campfire. Make that, Ben and I pitched the tents while Annabel and Lucy watched. Annabel had important hair braiding to do on Lucy, then Annabel had to excuse herself to the restroom area for another wardrobe change. Her wardrobe alone was the reason her backpack weighed twice as much as mine and Ben's combined—but luckily her hero, Ben, had offered to carry her bag for her. I like the guy, but this is getting sickening. I never offered to carry Lucy's backpack.

When I suggested to Annabel that she didn't seem like the camping type, Annabel informed me she went to summer camp two years in a row between third and fifth grades—"in Maine!"—and because of that hardship experience, she was quite capable of and qualified for an island wilderness adventure that included sleeping in a tent, so shut up, Wheaties. Sure she could survive—so long as Ben was in the tent next to hers! Maine, where? She's determined to prove she can make it through one night in the great outdoors, without her white-noise machine or her flatiron for hair touch-ups. Strangely, she's accomplished this without a sulk on her face the whole trip to Catalina. Stranger still, a year of sharing a bathroom with that girl back in Manhattan has taught me more than I ever wanted to know about hair-care products, and I'm man enough to admit I did borrow her climate-control hair gel when the island humidity popped my hair out to near 'fro level. Very useful product.

We were staying over for only one night, but Annabel made sure we wouldn't be caught unprepared for any wilderness emergency that might come up. In fact, the primary reason for the tonnage of her luggage here to Catalina wasn't all clothing—it was the giant, eleven-in-one "survival" lantern that, as the box said, came built with the following:

- ✓ Black-and-white TV, AM/FM weather-band radio, dual fluorescent lamps, spotlight, emergency siren, and red blinking light.
- ✓ LCD digital clock, thermometer, compass, sonic mosquito repeller, built-in handle, and retractable shoulder strap.
- ✓ All-in-one portable, lightweight case. (Ben may disagree.)

I give Annabel credit. That girl knew how to work Maurice so he'd let her use his credit card at The Sharper Image. I weep for the day Maurice realizes that encouraging Annabel to buy unnecessary gizmos for her so-called wilderness adventure will not only cost him a pretty penny, but will not buy him her respect. I weep further for the day Annabel finally watches Maurice's TV show that she declined to attend the taping of and realizes her Sharper Image adventure on Maurice's credit card somehow made it into the last-minute script changes for the episode in which Maurice takes the rebel nieces camping and none of them can survive without the expensive equipment they don't know how to use.

Where would we be without Annabel? Count on her to stake her own claim for an award in the Embarrass Wheaties competition. We sat around the campfire near our tents that night on Catalina, with Annabel and Ben sitting together on one side, Lucy next to me—but at a much farther distance than Annabel to Ben on the other side—and Tia sitting a short distance from our two boy-girl sets, like she was at the head of the table. Out of nowhere, Annabel asked Tia: "Do you want to have kids?"

The crackling of the fire did not distract from the Yet Even More Mortification I felt at Annabel's intrusive question. I have enough on my mind now! Why did Annabel have to bring up an issue I hadn't even thought to worry about before?

The marshmallow Tia was roasting on a stick collapsed into the fire before she answered. I must have felt the flush of embarrassment for her, because Tia's voice did not register any tone other than her usual mellow one. "Nah," Tia said. "I like it just like this—being with Al when he spends his school breaks with us in LA, hanging out with you kids at the campfire like now, or taking my nieces and nephews back home to Coney Island, that stuff, the fun stuff. I have no interest in the pain of childbirth or crying babies or the never-ending responsibility of worrying about my kid falling off a swing or not looking both ways before crossing the street. Then there's kids turning into teenagers. I love you all, but you guys with your minidramas—not for me. No offense. But I love small doses of the good times, like this."

Well, at least that's the procreation of one less future

half/step/whatever spawn I have to worry about. That's some compensation for the question being asked in the first place, *Annabel*.

Lucy blurted out, "No offense taken, Tia. I totally get it. I don't want a boyfriend. It's not that I don't like boys. It's that I like my time being my own right now. I'd rather have a boy who's a friend than a boy who's something more. Like it wouldn't be personal or anything." Lucy did not look at me, but I'm not so girl-challenged that I didn't know she had attempted to make up with me for not wanting to make out with me. On a scale of one to ten, I'd give her comment a five for how much it made me feel better—the still-hasn't-gone-away feeling of rejection prevented a higher score, but maybe by tomorrow or the next day the number will be more like a seven.

Chapter 18

Annabel

Finally! All the roasted marshmallows Tia ate made her sick to her stomach, trapping her in the bathroom. Fear of diarrhea and outdoor restroom facilities: the real reason I will never be caught dead camping again unless there's some form of Ben incentive involved.

The restroom area was far enough away from our tents to give me at least a half hour alone with Ben before she returned. Tia swore to Jack that her chaperoning responsibilities included her sleeping alongside me and Lucy in the girl tent while Ben and Wheaties slept in a separate tent, but what could Tia do if nature called? Saint Lucy went along with Tia to make sure she was okay, and Wheaties took off with my survival lantern to read his Sun-god book under a nearby tree. Hey, who's laughing about that supposedly unnecessary lantern now, Wheaties?

You know how there are some things you just *know*? I knew I wouldn't have to wait long for Ben to appear in my tent. I might not have much kissing experience with boys, but I knew enough to feel confident that the last few days of eye-flirting, secret smiles, and hand-holding when no one else could see us, had to lead somewhere—and soon, since Ben was returning to Australia the day after we would get home from Catalina. Sure enough, Tia and Lucy weren't five minutes gone from my tent, and Wheaties barely gone from swiping my lantern, when Ben popped his head through the zippered flap of the girls' tent.

"Madge, could I trouble you to borrow some antibacterial hand cleanser?" he asked, imitating Mom and Penny when they talk like they're housewives in a cleaning-product commercial, which is their little insider joke that no one besides them (and Maurice—'nuff said) thinks is funny.

The breath mint on my tongue dissolved right in time. "C'mon in," I said, trying to sound all husky and sexy. "*Mi* tent *es su* tent." Or more like, *mi* tent *es Señor Maurice's* tent—he bought us the most plush one on the market, probably because he was so desperate to have his new best friend, my mom, to himself for two days. I'm sure he remembers his promise to me and won't assume that just because I'm gone, he should move over from the couch he was sleeping on at Jack and Penny's to the one at Angelina's. That sleepover was a one-off deal, made possible in my good graces by

Ben's excitement over Maurice's presence, not mine.

Ben crawled into the tent and sat down on Lucy's sleeping bag, next to me. I couldn't see his face much except for the faint moonlight shining through the tent, beaming right onto his beautiful Ben eyes. Another thing I just knew, and his eyes told me he knew too, was the clock ticked against our time together until our chaperone, Tia, returned. I think I started to say something stupid like, "So what's up?" but he placed his index finger on my lip to shush me. The last time Ben and I had our moment together, in Melbourne, it was me who instigated The Kiss. This time, it was Ben who leaned in toward me, without either of us having to bother with small talk or that awkward Are We Gonna Do This Or Not time delay.

So, the Catalina kissing. Weird but graaayate. Weird because, well, it's weird to all of a sudden have another's person's *mouth* on yours, especially when the last time Ben's lips touched mine, it was more like an innocent peck where we smacked our lips against one another's for about five long, sweet, heart-thumping seconds, and then we separated, and that was that. This time, the lips probed instead of smacked, the stakes in the touching game feeling much higher. This time after the lip-touching got started, then hands-exploring got started too. But for all that difference from the last time, and the weirdness of knocking against his stubbly chin that was smooth as a baby's bottom last year, the graaayate part was, well, having not just another person's mouth on mine, but *Ben's*—the boy I had a whole secret box of artifacts devoted to, the boy from Oz I'd been dreaming about since my first trip to Australia!

The kissing was like a dream, just the way I had expected. I had the boy I wanted—oh, and a gorgeous one, thank you!—and as our lip-meeting really got going, after I got used to it, I felt that dreamy happiness you read about in books and think it's a phony lie, but now here I was, experiencing it.

But the difference in our ages since the first time we met back in Melbourne, and this night a year and a half later on Catalina, seemed to be much bigger for him than for me. Maybe I didn't have any experience since that innocent peck back in Melbourne, but there's no way Ben hadn't in the time since. I mean, his mouth and hands had moves you could only get from practice. They weren't learned from randomly flipping channels late at night and finding yourself unable to stop watching the freakfest that is those late night movies on the cable movie channels.

Another thing about kissing—it's complicated. Dude, I'm trying to breathe here! I was determined to stay in the game, though. I needed to have at least enough fooling-around experience with Ben to earn adequate I snagged an Aussie Footy God bragging rights once I start snob-girl high school in the fall. But I didn't expect it to be so hard to simultaneously be kissing my dream boy, enjoying it although it scared

me, while at the same time worrying about Tia returning, remembering to breathe through my nose, and
trying to subtly move Ben's hand from my stomach
back down to my hip without making it seem like I
wasn't into his hands either. But I managed. Complicated is good. I'm always up for a challenge.

I'm not sure which base we were on, but I was not
looking to steal extra bases. When his hand that I'd
just moved away from my stomach strayed from my
hip toward my thigh, my mind thought *uh-oh uh-oh
uh-oh*. That's when my brain revolted against me,
transmitting images of . . . my DAD! I will surely need
years of therapy now—Maurice better keep that credit
card available for me. Suddenly I understood why
Jack flipped out at me for wearing that outfit the day
we first saw Ben. It was about more than censoring my
fashion statement. Jack hadn't been trying to hold me
back from something *he* wasn't ready for me to have
yet—he was trying to hold me back from an experience maybe *I* wasn't ready for yet.

I wanted the kissing to stop, only I didn't. Complicated is confusing. I wanted the romantic part—the
flirting, the anticipation, the first touch of lips—to go
on forever, but where the kissing led now was more
like too many steps forward, and I kinda wanted to
take two steps back. The deep kissing felt like too
much world opening up to me, in a situation that
could only end with me being in doubt: What was
going too far with a boy who lived in faraway Aus-

tralia? Would I see him again? Talk to him again? It was like I had opened the door expecting to just peek inside at this new world, but then those doors flung wide open, and all I wanted was to slam them shut.

Maybe Wheaties had that psychic thing going and knew about me and my needing the door to that world closed, because the loud siren on my survival lantern that he'd taken blared out once, loud and startling enough for Ben to remove his body from mine with all-star footy-boy speed.

"Tia's coming back," Ben whispered. "I told Wheaties to accidentally on purpose set off the siren if he saw her and Lucy heading back." Bam! Ben was gone from my tent. Yeah, that boy definitely has more experience than he lets on.

HEY! Ben had Wheaties be his point person so Ben could make the moves on me! I wasn't sure whether to be flattered or annoyed. Mostly, I was relieved. At least Ben's pawn boy had put an end to our strange-lovely-confusing tent of kissing world.

Probably we all wanted an end to the tent world. Later that night, the skies opened and we woke up soaked, freezing and miserable. Tia's tummy still ached, and Miss Crosswell had awoken well cross herself. Lucy glared at me for what reason I don't know. Had I snored at night? Or did she know something happened between me and Ben, and she was mad I hadn't told her (how could I with Tia there)?

I'd been so excited to be on Catalina with Ben, and now I couldn't wait to leave! Once again, Tia made my secret hope possible. She made the executive decision for us to take the early boat home to LA. Like a good ex-New Yorker, Tia moaned, "I've had it with this outdoors business. We saw enough pretty stuff yesterday. Can't get back to the city fast enough."

I hadn't called Mom to tell her we were coming home early, so I got a little surprise when I walked through the door after Tia dropped me off. As I stepped into the living room, who did I bump into but Maurice—wearing only a towel around his waist—coming out of the steamed-up bathroom. My eyes will never recover from the hairy-beast vision, which will probably now require a lifetime of counseling for me.

Angelina followed behind him, wearing a robe. I might as well move in with a shrink at this point. "Oh!" she said when she saw me. "I wasn't expecting you home until this evening."

Sulking would not communicate the proper venom of my feeling at this moment. "Get out!" I said to Maurice. More like, yelled. Truce: OVER.

"It's not what you think," Angelina said. "He stayed over and helped take care of Ariel while I slept. She was up all night and I was exhausted, so Maurice came by since he doesn't sleep at night anyway. Nothing happened here, Annabel, besides Maurice getting stuck changing nappies and fixing bottles all night. And I don't like your tone, young lady. How dare you make assumptions about Maurice and me? You need to learn to trust me about these things."

Tone schmone, trust schmust. "Nappies are called diapers here, Angelina," I said. "You're not an Australian. Not one yet."

I should have known better than to trust the promise of an Australian unfunny comedy troll. I went to my bedroom and slammed the door shut for real. Now it was my turn to feel sick to my stomach. I reached for the bedroom telephone. I knew just the doctor to call to fix all our problems.

Chapter 19

Lucy

Maybe it's the feminine troubles that struck for real this morning, but sweet little Lucy woke up in a rage. For one thing, that other song Mum and Dad sing together besides the annoying one about nobody walking in LA, the song about how ♪ *it never rains in Southern California* ♪, is apparently a big fat lie.☹ Maurice spent a zillion dollars on our tent, but either he bought one with a gaping hole in it (possible) or Wheaties popped a hole in it by mistake when pitching it (more likely). Guess which lucky person in the girls' tent woke up at the crack of dawn because of a hard drip drip drip splattering directly onto her face? That's right, me. Couldn't the tent-roof hole have been carved over Annabel, since her sleep mask might have served as an umbrella against the cold rain? As if the rain wasn't bad enough, guess who else got to wake up to that time of the month? Annabel worries all the time about not being "developed" enough in the boobs area, but I'd give back all my so-called development and my overflowing B cup not to wake up with (1) a rain-soaked face, (2) cramps, and (3) well, you know. Yuck. Stupid island getaway.

Annabel woke up next to me, breathing her foul morning breath onto my left side, but she was already on my bad side. Not only did she stick me with looking after Tia last night—which I didn't mind, really, as we couldn't let Tia go off to be sick on her own, but I thought making sure Tia was okay should be Annabel's responsibility as much as mine—but when Tia and I returned to the tent, Annabel didn't even bother to tell me what did or didn't happen with Ben while we were gone. That lantern siren Wheaties "accidentally" blared when Tia and I came back round the camp area? So not subtle.

Our gang was supposed to go on an underwater sea adventure today before heading back to LA this evening, but that got canceled after Annabel's morning whining about the rain and cold (and she wasn't the one that got directly rained on in her sleep!), and then Tia deciding that we were done with Catalina country and should skip the planned adventure to go home early. The brochure for the glass bottom boat had promised: *Sit five feet under the water in a spacious, climate-controlled cabin and watch Catalina's abundant marine life. As we feed the fish, you'll come face-to-face with a wide array of undersea dwellers: bright orange garibaldi, spotted calico bass, opaleye, halfmoons, urchins, rockfish, and bat rays.* It had been all I could do not to tell Angus about this boat so he wouldn't be jealous of our Catalina trip. I had a secret plan to inspect this boat to determine whether it was a worthy suggestion to Mum and Dad for a place to celebrate Angus's next birthday.

Our canceled undersea boat adventure ruined something else I had planned to celebrate, privately: my real dad's birthday. He would have been forty today. He would have liked me celebrating him on an underwater boat looking at marine life. All I wanted for this day was that it be a sunny, warm one like back in Australia, and I could remember the weekends when I was little, when Daddy and I rode the tram to St. Kilda before going sailing on Port Philip Bay. Since my memories were private, I had planned to sit by myself in the lower deck of the glass bottom boat, hugging my knees to my chest like Mum, watching all the fish swim around, and maybe I would put headphones on my ears so no one would try to talk to me; the sounds I would hear would be my memory playing back my dad's voice, explaining to me about the different fish species.

Instead, I rode the rain-swept ferry back to Long Beach, shivering in my soaked jeans and shirt with my dirt-splattered wet hair making me feel almost frozen, and got trapped with the rat pack of step-whatevers who I am seriously sick of right now! Oh, the glamour!

Wheaties sat next to me on the inside ferry deck, coughing. He said, "We should have prepared for rain. Why didn't we think to do that? I'm very prone to illness. I hope I don't get sick."

"What's this?" I answered. "After the last few days of virtual silent treatment from you, now I'm good enough to be talked to again? Oh, I'm sorry, Wheaties, I can't be bothered today to care whether or not you get sick from the rain and the cold."

No more Saint Lucy today. I've tried so hard to be nice to him since that weird incident at the cinema, and I am sick of trying. I don't owe it to Wheaties to be attracted to him. Why should I feel bad about tossing his unwelcome hand from my shoulder? I didn't do anything wrong—*he* did!

Annabel returned from the ferry concession stand where Ben stood in line buying her a hot chocolate. She sat herself down beside me, uninvited, on the seat that Wheaties had just vacated. What a hypocrite she's become since Ben's arrival! She doesn't even like hot chocolate from a mix. She'll only drink the kind made by her Bubbe with Ghirardelli cocoa, organic milk, and real, not dried, marshmallows floating on top. I've had Bubbe's hot cocoa and it's quite good—that's one standard worth holding high. But throw Annabel's boy crush into the mixture, and all of a sudden her standards were nonexistent. And how come my rain-soaked hair was dirty and limp, while hers managed to look curly and elegant, as if her daughter-of-Angelina dark blond tresses were surprised by the rain, but could make do in a perfectly fashionable way against all this damp adversity?

Annabel cupped her hand around my ear and whispered into it, "Thanks for covering with Tia last night. Want to hear what happened?" She giggled. Her hot breath against my cold ear only made me madder.

With a shoulder shrug, I knocked her hand from my ear. I shot her back a giggle-free, stone-cold face. "No, I don't really want to hear, and I didn't appreciate being made the point person last night, either." You'd think she would have been properly insulted by my comment, but then Ben the dreamy boy wonder appeared in front of us. He held out a Styrofoam cup of poor-quality hot chocolate for her, and she forgot all about me and my newfound Annabel-brand of bad mood. Something happened last night between her and Ben, that's for sure. Too bad how I've decided I'm not interested.

"Thanks, Ben!" Annabel squealed. She patted the empty seat on her other side. "Come sit by me!" Now I got up. I was seriously going to chunder. I am rapidly losing respect for her. My Annabel nausea started when she forgot about the example she's supposed to be setting for Angus, who looks up to her as a fellow vegetarian, and she ate meat instead of a vegi-dog that day at Pink's—all because Ben thinks girls who slurp down chili dogs are hot. Now here she was grabbing for hot chocolate made from the same mix that she turns her nose up at when my mum offers it to her. Annabel is the total example of why I'm not in a rush to have a boyfriend. I'm not about to go changing just so some boy I like will like me back. How could I ever be sure the guy really liked me if I hadn't even let him get to know the real me, whoever she is?

When we got home to LA, for once I was glad Annabel had her own house up the hill and didn't want to stay over at our house. Patrick and his girlfriend might be sleeping in my bedroom until they return to Australia, but I would gladly sleep on the floor in Angus's room rather than share Annabel's room with her up the street tonight. Saint Lucy, RIP. When I thought about it, I had been very nice about being willing to share my room with Annabel when she came to LA, but why should I have been? Princess doesn't even want to share my room, so this lady-in-waiting has decided that Annabel's open invitation to share my room is: Officially. Withdrawn. And as soon as Annabel brings it up, I'll be sure to let her know that.

For now, it will be my secret, like the secret of my real dad's birthday that Mum must have forgotten all about, because when we got home, Mum was slow dancing with Jack to the R&B station on the radio—in the middle of the kitchen! Aside from there being no reason whatsoever to be dancing in the middle of the house on a rainy day, shouldn't Mum have been with Angus, showing him pictures of our real dad and making sure Angus celebrated him on this special day? At least she sent Angus to the right place for the day. Patrick and his girlfriend had offered to take Angus and Bebe to the aquarium so Mum and Dad could have some time alone together. That's great that the oldies wanted some time for themselves, but I honestly think today was not the appropriate day for that.

The house did feel strangely empty, with just Mum and Dad and their slow dance to the pretty melody in the kitchen, and me taking on the Annabel sulk role, alone in my room. With Bebe and Angus out and Ben having decided to hang out at Wheaties' for the day to watch videos, I almost didn't know what to do, being all alone for the first time in a long time and having my bedroom to myself.

Sulking in private grows boring quickly without anyone there to make miserable by it. This must be the secret to Annabel's success with it.

I sat at my desk and took out the scrapbook I had made with my Granny Nell in Melbourne, my book of memories of my dad. The book contained pages of his photos from the time he was a baby, to him holding me as a baby, to him patting Mum's tummy with baby Angus inside. Along with the photos, Granny Nell and I had filled the pages with drawings he had made, stories he had written when he was a kid, and some letters he had written to Granny Nell from boarding school about how he loved his science courses and how he intended to study marine biology at university.

I think my real dad would have liked Jack. He would be happy that Mum found someone so nice and that Angus and I got a good dad since our natural one could only look out for us from Heaven. He'd probably even like Princess Annabel, just maybe not today. Maybe if his job had transferred him to LA, maybe like me, he'd really love Southern California, but sometimes break down just a little from being surrounded by loud people with grating accents, their strange, oversized foods, and their arrogant, foreign ways. Just sometimes he would melt down from missing Australia and Melbourne, from missing the places and people he loved and understood.

I was so engrossed looking through the scrapbook, I didn't hear Rapunzel herself knocking on my bedroom window until her knock turned into a BANG against the glass. I raised the window. "Why don't you just come in through the regular door?" I said.

Annabel said, "Don't feel like talking to anybody. Besides you." I was still irritated with her, but I held out my hands to help lift her through the window anyway. She squeezed some rain from her long hair and the drips landed on the scrapbook I'd placed on my desk, directly onto a picture of Josephine Snickercross that my dad had drawn for me when I was in kindie.

"Watch it!" I said. I grabbed some Kleenex to blot the water from the precious page. I barely saved the fancy swirling lettering that Daddy had drawn of the words "Josephine Snickercross" from smearing.

Annabel looked at the scrapbook. "*That's* Josephine?" she said. "From hearing you and Angus whisper about her, I thought she was a real person, not a fairy person."

I grabbed the book and placed it on the top bunk, out of her view.

"Don't talk about Josephine," I said. "You have no right."

"What's that supposed to mean?" She sat down at my desk and crossed her arms over her chest. "Are you saying you don't want me knowing about your secret family code because I'm not your real family?"

"I didn't say that!"

"You act like it."

How exactly did we get to this point of a near fight, anyway? Saint Lucy came back from the dead and decided we should talk about something else. I said, "What are you doing here? I thought you were going to take a long hot bath at your house and then go over Wheaties' to hang out with him and Ben this afternoon."

"Plan changed," Annabel said. "I came home to find stupid Maurice had spent the night."

"He's not really stupid, Annabel. Dad says he tested like a 140 IQ or something. Mum said it's his emotional IQ that's the problem . . ."

"The problem," Annabel interrupted me, "is that YOUR family had to bring him here from YOUR country to ruin MY family."

"What are you talking about?" So this is what the boiling point felt like—so mad and sick of accommo-

198

dating her moods that if she didn't back down now, I couldn't be held accountable for what I might say to her.

She didn't bother toning down her voice. She all-out yelled at me like she'd been taking voice lessons from Patrick's girlfriend. "YOU GUYS MOVING TO LA HAS RUINED EVERYTHING FOR ME!"

And here was where my boiling point met boiling over. I yelled back at her, "YOU BEING HERE MAKES EVERYONE ELSE MISERABLE! YOU THINK THE WORLD REVOLVES AROUND YOU! THERE ARE OTHER PEOPLE IN THIS FAMILY WITH FEELINGS, PRINCESS, SO GET OVER YOURSELF!"

Her face registered a moment of shock. I guess she didn't know Saint Lucy was capable of her own temper tantrum. Then she stomped out of my room, through the bedroom door and not the window. She didn't bother taking her case to Mum and Dad in the kitchen, because within seconds, I heard the front door of our house slam.

From my bedroom window I watched Annabel march back up the street toward her own house. I heard the front door slam a second time and saw Dad run after Annabel. When he caught up with her, he took her hand and continued walking up the street with her. Annabel thinks she's the mature one, but I think she's the stepsister who can be spoiled and igno-rant—she doesn't even know to appreciate the simple gift of having her dad available to her.

Mum came into my room and touched my shoulder from behind me. In that soothing, mum kind of voice, she asked, "What happened here, Luce? What was the shouting about?"

The wetness on my face did not come from the rain splattering through the open window, and it wasn't even specks of tears I could control. No, I got a flood bursting through my eyes, along with the horrible wheeze-sobs that come from nowhere and refuse to be controlled.

Mum placed my head on her shoulder and pulled me close, patting my hair and then kissing the top of my head while all that . . . stuff . . . came out. When the crying settled, she pulled back and touched her fingers to my chin so I'd look her in the eyes. "Feels good to let out a big cry sometimes, hey Luce?" I nodded and she pulled me back to her, and my face found its place on her shoulder again, tired. "You don't always have to be so nice, you know. It's okay to get angry sometimes, to let it all out. Want to talk about it?" My shaking head ground NO into her shoulder. I was mad at Annabel, but I didn't want Mum being mad at her too. What happened between me and Annabel was between just us two. I wiped my nose on Mum's blouse.

Mum reached for the Kleenex, then took my hand and guided me to sit on the bottom bunk. She sat down next to me, the scrapbook in her hands. I leaned against her and she put her arm around my shoulder, and I did not have one instinct to shrug her hand away. Mum said, "I'd planned to have some time with you and Angus alone tonight after you got back from Catalina, so we could talk about Daddy, remember him. But maybe now would be a better time, hey? Just us two—the girls who along with Granny Nell knew and loved him best? Maybe we can get Granny Nell in Melbourne on the phone too? I know that's a person whose voice you'd like to hear right now—and she, your voice, especially today."

I nodded, sniffled, and wiped my nose on her shoulder again.

"That would be dinkum," I said.

Chapter 20

WHEATIES

I didn't want to, but Ben and Tia agreed if we were going to spend a rainy pizza-and-videos day inside at the Westwood apartment, we should invite Annabel and Lucy to join us. Misery loves company, said Tia.

Our family is getting out of control with codependency. I, for one, could be miserable just fine on my own without Lucy being around. Her message: I GOT IT, ALREADY.

Maybe I deserved her snapping at me on the boat back from Catalina, I don't know. I'm thinking about it. Maybe since the Moment of Mortification at The Grove with Lucy, I have been practicing on Lucy the affliction called passive-aggressiveness that Tia says I need to work on.

I wouldn't get the chance to work on it with Lucy

today, however, as misery preferred its own homes today. When I called Angelina's house to invite the girls over, Angelina told me, "Al, honey, you guys have fun on your own today. Annabel and I had a spat this morning, and Penny just called to tell me Annabel and Lucy had a big fight, so maybe a little time-out is in order. This will all pass, I'm sure, but today is probably not the day for you four to hang out. But Ariel and I are looking forward to the La Brea Tar Pits later this week with you!" She made smooching sounds into the phone like I've never once heard my real mom do with me, and said good-bye.

Misery is curious to know whether this visitation situation with Angelina is going to be a permanent one. Are Dad and I going to become that family—fractured not once by the distance of Mom and Tia living in LA but yet again by Angelina-Annabel-Ariel living separately from us? Am I going to measure my half-sister's growth from baby to toddler to kid by limited viewings of her at like museums during school breaks? Who will I rely on for secret hair-care product tips without Annabel to share a bathroom with?

"I love LA," Ben said as he hooked the Xbox into the living room TV. "Do you think you could live here permanently instead of New York? I would live here in a—what's that Annabel says—New York minute?"

"I don't think I could live permanently in LA," I said. "I would want to be where my dad is, and he would never live here. Unless he's on vacation, the farthest he ever wants to go from Manhattan is, like, Connecti-cut."

Ben said, "Have no idea what or where a Connecticut is."

"You're not missing anything," I assured him.

I thought I wasn't mad about Mom missing out on the rainy day in Westwood, since I knew she would not get home until very late at night. Then it occurred to me that for the first time since she'd moved to LA, I had an actual friend to show off here, and maybe she should be home to see that the friend in fact does exist, even if that risked her embarrassing me in front of Ben.

Tia came into the living room, tossing me a DVD. She said, "Yo, Al, catch this. I think we should watch *Sixteen Candles* first, and then we can follow that with this cable TV show called *The Dead Zone* I've been saving to show you. I got a whole double-bill experiment worked out. See, *Sixteen Candles* has a teenage actor named Anthony Michael Hall in it who plays a character called 'The Geek.'"

"Tia!" I stammered, not liking where this was going. I picked the DVD up from the spot where it fell when I missed the catch.

"No wait, Al, listen up. The Geek wins the prom queen! Great moral of the story, right? Oh, did I just ruin the movie? Nah. But you've really gotta see how Anthony Michael Hall goes from that movie to how he looks as an adult in *The Dead Zone*, an all bulked up, manly hottie."

"I've seen *Weird Science*, Tia. I know all about Anthony Michael Hall. And I don't think Ben wants to spend his last full day in America having an Anthony Michael Hall film festival."

Tia's face fell. She looked toward Ben. "You wouldn't?"

Ben said, "Not to be rude or anything, Tia, but honestly . . . no!"

Tia said, "You boys have no taste. I don't like video games, so I'm going online to one of those Anthony Michael Hall fan sites and have fun by myself. Come get me when you're ready to order the pizza."

Ben tossed me a player console after Tia left the room. He said, "Tia has strange tastes. But she's all right."

Ben's a foreigner so I guess that's why he's not aware of the rules here: (1) He should have been weird about the Mom-Tia situation and not wanted to hang out here today, and (2) in the American high school universe, he would be too cool to be hanging out with me at all on a rainy day. He could easily spend today having girls fawning all over him at the mall, or he could be at the arcade high-fiving with the skater dudes. Maybe they have different rules in Australia, or maybe it's just Ben—I don't know. Australians are confusing me lately. I'm not going to develop a case of hero worship on him or anything, because the rules clearly state that would be pathetic. But if Ben ever wants to go to college in America, I will personally volunteer to coach him through his SATs, free of charge, no worries.

I know the rules also say I'm not supposed to gossip like a girl with my unexpected Aussie buddy, but I was curious about what happened on Catalina. I kicked his leg while we played Grand Theft Auto and asked him, "So what's the deal with Annabel? Is she your girl-friend now?"

"Dude," Ben said. "She's your sister. Don't you know I can't talk to you about that? There are rules about these things, Wheaties." So something definitely did happen while I got stuck being the sidekick point person, or he wouldn't be not telling. He kicked at my ankle. "And what about you, mate?"

I don't know where my guts all of a sudden came from, but I said, "I kinda liked Lucy but she didn't like me back, and now I kinda think I don't know if we can be friends anymore."

It felt like such a huge big deal to admit that, but Ben only laughed. He said, "Lucy's a girl. She doesn't know what she wants! Play it cool with her. Let her relax enough to get to know you better. Act like you couldn't care less whether she notices you that way. And give it some time. Next summer, you wait and see—she'll look at you differently after all the time and distance you've invested in ignoring her. Isn't that what your friend Mr. Machiavelli would advise? Be patient, until the time is right to take your stand— or something?"

Maybe it will be Ben coaching me on my SATs, not the other way around. Who knew the sporty creature was capable of so much wisdom, like one day there could be a new Mount Rushmore, profiling the man-geniuses of Machiavelli, Sun Tzu, Ben—and Anthony Michael Hall, if it's Tia doing the stone carving.

Tia came back into the room and handed me the phone. "Your mom wants to tell you something," she said.

I took the phone. Mom said, "Alan, I'm sorry I'm missing meeting your friend, but I have a big SEC fil-ing that needs to be ready by tomorrow. But invite Ben to spend the night if he wants. I might be home by midnight, and I'd love the chance to say hi to him before he goes back to Australia."

Maybe because I was feeling good that I was whup-ping Ben on the video game, but for once I said to Mom what I really thought. "If you really want to know the people in my life, Mom, start with me. Let your associates do the work today, and you get your butt home and learn about the possible litigious aspects of carpal tunnel syndrome caused by too many games of Grand Theft Auto. You're the boss—you're allowed to play hooky. I'm your son and I'm only here for so long. Either be in this or don't." Passive aggres-sive is so over. Signor Machiavelli: take note.

A long silence came from her end of the phone; then Mom sounded surprised when she said, "You'd actually want me to play hooky and spend the day with you, Alan?"

Now it was my turn to be surprised. "Sure, why

not," I said. "It'd be graayate." I handed the phone back to Tia, who flashed me a very un-Tia-like, un-mellow grin.

"Good job," Tia mouthed at me.

It's like that guy Sun Tzu says: "To fight and conquer in all your battles is not supreme excellence; supreme excellence consists in breaking the enemy's resistance without fighting."

Chapter 21

Ben

Annabel and I arranged it on the boat back from Catalina: On my last afternoon in America, I would say I wanted to go for a hike up the canyon while Dad and Miss Shouty had their last sacred star-map driving adventure, and Annabel would meet me at the canyon crest at the designated time so we could say our good-byes in private. Like, private-private, not just the whispered "good-bye, I'll write you, I'll miss you" empty good-bye. Something—I don't know what, but *something*—got started in that tent when Tia and Lucy were gone, and I reckoned we had to see where to finally leave it off, before I returned to Oz and Annabel to New York.

How *something* got started at all, I'm still unclear on. First I was disinterested in her as the weird punk girl, then I warmed to her when she became the relaxed fun girl, then against my better judgment I really wanted to get cozy with the flirty posh girl—but I didn't come to America expecting to get *something* going at all. I don't know what came over me that night on Catalina, but I couldn't stop myself from going into Annabel's tent to find out if all that buzz between her various personalities and me ought to move up a level.

The elevated level of getting to know one another was all right. Not great, not terrible. It was almost sweet, although her lips and body felt unsure about it at the time. Annabel sure let go of me super quick when Wheaties blared the siren, practically shoving me off her, which was strange considering her minty fresh breath when I stepped inside that tent, indicating she definitely wanted *something* to happen. So when she suggested in my ear on the boat ride back from Catalina that we meet up on the canyon before I left, so we could have a "special" good-bye, I said, "You're sure?" thinking she was so not sure, but she answered, "Yeah, I thought about it after you left. And I could definitely use more practice in certain areas if you know what I mean, and I think you are just the coach." That breed of New York girl is bold. I like it. Any decent coach will tell you that superior playing skills don't come out of nowhere—they're all about discipline and regular practice. Who would I be to say no to Annabel's request to diligently follow through with playing practice?

You'd think a simple canyon hike would not be a

big deal to go off and do on your own. Wrong. I almost suspected a conspiracy brewed to keep me and her from having our secret good-bye. Miss Shouty kept holding me up before I could leave for the hike, coming in to the living room to check on my packing progress: "DO YOU HAVE EXTRA ROOM IN YOUR LUGGAGE FOR SOME OF THE GIFTS I BOUGHT? YOU'LL BE BACK FROM YOUR HIKE LONG BEFORE FIVE O'CLOCK, RIGHT? YOU'RE SURE YOUR DAD HAS YOUR PASSPORT?" Then Angus wanted me to read The Book with him. Then Penny wanted me to help her make sandwiches for us to take on the plane ride back home. If Annabel's father hadn't been away at his office, I might have suspected him of leading all the obstruction to my hike.

When I was finally ready to leave Jack and Penny's house to take the walk on my own, it occurred to me that something suspicious was going on with Lucy. She'd hardly emerged from her bedroom now that Dad and Miss Shouty were packed and vacated from it, and she loves a canyon hike more than anybody does—it's she who introduced me and Annabel to it. Why hadn't she asked to tag along?

I knew it was a mistake to check on her before leaving the house, but she's my countrywoman, so I had to. I knocked on her partially open door, and when she didn't answer, I opened the door all the way to see Lucy lying on her bottom bunk bed, her feet against the wall, with headphones on her ears. When she saw me, she took off the headphones, and I saw that her eyes were red from crying. I *knew* I shouldn't have come in here first.

"What's the matter?" I asked. I hoped she could tell me quickly so I could offer some lightning-fast make-it-all-better Ben wisdom that I should seriously charge a fee to dole out, I'm getting so good. Then I could get up the canyon for the good-bye "practice" with Annabel before our time officially ran out.

"Annabel and I had a fight," Lucy said. "We haven't talked since we got back from Catalina. Even when I lived in Australia and she was in New York, we never went more than twenty-four hours without at least talking on the computer."

"So who was wrong and who was right?"

She shrugged. "I don't know. Both of us and neither of us."

I looked at my watch. I was so late at this point that by the time I met up with Annabel, we'd barely have fifteen minutes alone up there, unless I sprinted up the canyon. "You'll work it out," I assured Lucy. I stepped away, prepared to bolt, but that head irritation called a conscience made me stop, pause, sigh in defeat, and take two steps forward, back inside Lucy's room. Sacrifices are brutal. "Why don't you come on this hike with me and tell big brother Ben all about it?"

Lucy got up. "You're not my brother and I'm not sure I even understand the fight with Annabel enough to tell you about it, but I would love to go on the hike with you. I haven't left the house since we got back from Catalina, and I'm getting sick of staring at the four walls of this bedroom."

What was I gonna do? If I wasn't going to get the last minutes alone with Annabel to settle once and for all whether she should be my American girlfriend or whatever, I could at least get the two girl halves of The Quads talking again. International diplomacy and all. I couldn't leave knowing that two stepsisters who seem to me to be more like real sisters, who would be miserable without each other, hadn't made up—even if it meant I wouldn't be making out. I should be so lucky to have a step or half or someone that cared about me like Lucy and Annabel care about each other. That would be the only benefit of any Dad/Miss Shouty permanent union, except if they had a kid, I'd probably be old enough to be its granddad instead of its brother by the time it was born. But it might be interesting getting to know that genetically linked little person.

Annabel's impatient-girl personality waited for me at the canyon crest. From a distance, I could see her looking at her watch and pacing around the park bench while looking for me. Her face brightened when she saw me approach, then immediately darkened to storm cloud when she saw Lucy trailing behind me. When she saw Annabel, Lucy Crosswell's face expressed its own displeasure at me for double-crossing her.

"Hey," I told Annabel.

"Hey," she said back, then crossed her arms over her chest, with a face turned to vintage sulk. "I thought you were coming by yourself." I don't know how she does it—the sulk face is hot on her. I really must like her because most girls when they sulk just make me want to be full-body-dipped in Vegemite rather than deal with their moods.

I announced to the girls, "I'm taking a jog halfway back down the canyon to where the doggie fountain is. Don't either of you dare meet me at that point until you've worked out whatever the problem is."

"But . . . ," they both sputtered.

I threw my hand up. "Don't want to hear it," I said. I took off in a gallop-sprint that they could never catch up to. I wasn't kidding about not wanting to hear about the problem. Girl drama could go on for hours if I let them drag me into it. I just wanted them to work it out. Done deal.

Once I reached the doggie fountain, I waited a good twenty minutes for them, worrying with each passing minute that not only would they not work it out, but them not working it out would cause me to be very late getting back to the house to leave for the airport. Then I'd really have a problem—with Miss Shouty—to work out. But I also figured, hey, Miss Shouty had caused me to spend the first week of my California vacation waiting in queues for her tourist adventure I had wanted no part of, so if she had to sweat out a few extra minutes worrying about us making our plane on time, I could live with that. I needn't have worried too much, though, because soon Annabel and Lucy emerged down the canyon, their pinkie fingers latched to each other's, with red faces either from crying or hiking, I'm not sure which.

"Everything okay?" I asked.

"Yeah," they both said.

Annabel dropped Lucy's hand and took mine in its place. My *something* girl wasn't going to let me go without some kind of touching. I reckon that's all right. Lucy said, "You guys go on by yourselves. I'll hang out here a little before going back home."

What a sport. But Annabel said, "No, Luce. Where we go, you go. Plus, Dad said we can't do the canyon walk alone—but luckily Angelina didn't know that rule when I left our house to come here."

So that was that. After all the planning and wondering what would happen, Annabel and I would have no time alone to figure *something* out after all. Whatever *something* is between us, it is what it is. *Something* will figure itself out once I get back to Australia and Annabel and I have IMs and e-mails and digital photos to communicate with—until next (American) summer, that is. I wouldn't have minded one last private lippy conference, but that was the price of my sacrifice.

When we reached the bottom of the canyon back in front of Lucy's house, we found Dad and Miss Shouty waiting for me in the rental car. Her Loudness rolled down the passenger-side window and said, "YOU'RE LATE! DO YOU WANT US TO MISS OUR PLANE? WE'VE BEEN WORRIED SICK WONDERING WHERE YOU WERE."

I said, "The hike took a little longer than I expected. Sorry, Birdy."

Birdy's mouth dropped open. For once, the shouty lady whose voice is anything but soothing birdlike was speechless. Even Dad looked stunned. Finally Birdy said, "Good God, that's the first time you've ever addressed me by name."

"Had to happen sometime, Birdy," I said, thinking *if you had a normal name like Linda or something, I might have started long before now.*

Who cared what anyone thought I would do? I know they never expected my last stand on American soil to be my declaration of . . . er . . . public affection for the moody girl, but what the hey. I leaned down and kissed Annabel good-bye—on the lips no less, very fast and innocently, but in front of everyone, for all to see.

Something may have future potential.

Chapter 22

Annabel

I am loving all Australians right now, what can I say? Even Maurice Jackson has a temporary stay of execution in my heart. Since he is an Australian (all of whom, by the way, I repeat, I am loving loving loving), I've decided to believe him, that he was just helping out Angelina with Ariel and that he would never break his promise to me. Just because I've decided to believe the Australian, doesn't mean it's not time for him to bow out of our lives till Mom figures things out. I mean, he's got a supposed hot career that should be sucking up his time right now, even if he is convinced of his career's failure.

Bubbe arrived just in time to clean up this mess. Well, almost in time. She did miss meeting Ben. Bubbe and Ben probably could have waved to each other from their planes at LAX, him leaving and her arriving. No worries. I have plenty of new additions to the Ben box, proof of his existence and of our time together these last couple weeks, to show Bubbe later, and show her and show her and show her: tons of new pix from our adventures around LA, which since he likes this place, I have decided I like it too, and Ben's footy T-shirt that I may never wash, swiped from his backpack on the ride back from Catalina while he was getting me that poor-quality hot chocolate.

I wonder if I am in love. Now that I'm used to the kissing, I think I'd like more of it—a lot more. Is there a snob-girl high school in Melbourne where I could do an exchange program? My mission now is clear—figure out how to con Jack and Angelina into sending me to Australia, and SOON. Lucy and Angus are going this Christmas to see their Granny Nell, so maybe if I promise to give up sulking for at least the rest of the summer, the way some people give up candy for Lent, maybe my parents will agree to let me go to Melbourne with The Steps. Hey, I can dream.

News! I think I may be filling out my A cup. Life is GOOD again, my dread fading away. Having Bubbe here in LA, I get that same feeling I get in NY when I'm on the crosstown bus leaving the boring Upper East Side, that huge feeling of relief that passes through me as the bus emerges from leafy Central Park to reveal the stately, possibly haunted, buildings on Central Park West on the Upper West Side—the best side, our family's side.

After I called her, Bubbe flew out here the next day. She dragged Harvey with her whether he wanted to come or not. One way or the other, Bubbe said, Angelina and Harvey needed to settle their marriage. Once she'd deposited Harvey at our rental house, Bubbe decided she and I should spend a day on our own together, shopping at Bloomingdale's and then seeing a movie like we do back in NYC, while Harvey and Angelina talked it out.

Bubbe had only been in LA for a day and already she missed New York, so that's why she chose Cantor's Deli for us to have lunch. It's a Jewish deli like in New York, but with palm trees outside and skinnier people with fake body parts eating at the tables, but pretty much the same food and the same cheesy pictures of celebrities from a million years ago on the walls. The place smelled right, too, like corned beef and pickles, and Bubbe's summer linen suit scented by cigarettes and Chanel No. 19.

I sat at Bubbe's side rather than opposite her at the restaurant booth as we stared out the glass windows at the traffic and the plastic people going by on the street. Bubbe put her arm around my shoulder. She said, "And why is it that my bonus grandchild Lucy chose not to join us on this outing today, even though I personally called to invite her along with us?"

You know what "generation gap" really means? It means stuff you'll tell your grandma that you'd never tell your mom. I told Bubbe, "Lucy and I had a big fight. Then Ben forced us to make up from the fight, and we did and that was good. But Lucy and I have spent so much time together this summer, I think she needed a break from Steps today, to like do stuff with Angus and Bebe."

"What started the fight?"

"I'm not sure exactly. I was mad at Mom. And sometimes I get kinda mad that Lucy gets Jack all the time."

"Mad," Bubbe asked, "or jealous?"

"Jealous," I admitted. "Sometimes I look at what they have, and it's like I think they stole what should be mine. Even though I know Jack and Angelina were never going to make it, and I really like Penny and The Steps, sometimes I crack a little and I want what they have, and I get sad that they have it and I don't. Plus Angelina and Harvey are a mess, and that means everything is a mess for me and Wheaties, too." After the fight with Lucy, when Jack followed me from their house, we ended up going to a diner nearby and having a long talk, just us two. Dad told me that my fight with Lucy was what happens in families—but we could work together to work it out. And if I would consider staying at their house more, I would see that. I didn't tell Bubbe that part because she's like Angelina—glad for me to be close to my dad, but worried about me wanting to live with him permanently. "But Bubbe?"

"Yes?"

I try to be mature and sophisticated and everything, but with Bubbe I don't feel like I have to hold back the not-so-nice part of me. I told her, "I did a bad thing. When Lucy and I had that fight, I didn't realize the reason she was upset was because it was her real dad's birthday. I had no idea. Jack told me later. I feel really awful about that. I was mad at Lucy for having something I don't, and maybe she was mad at me for the same thing."

"Did you apologize to Lucy?"

"I did, but not until Ben made me talk to her again. It shouldn't have taken a boy I like and wanted to impress to make me do the right thing. I wanted to say sorry so badly to Lucy, but I thought she was so mad at me that she wouldn't even talk to me. I should have been big enough to do it anyway. If Ben hadn't made us talk again, we might still be mad."

"I doubt that. You two will always find your way back to each other. You're sisters. And next time you'll know not to let your pride get in the way when you owe someone an apology?"

I nodded. "But when Lucy and I made up, it turned out she had felt the same way I had—sorry about what happened, but worried I wouldn't talk to her. So I'm not the only guilty party, and hopefully she learned her lesson too." I slurped up some of Bubbe's egg-cream soda. "Bubbe, I will be glad when this summer is over!"

"*Oysgeshpilt*," Bubbe said, then translated: "You're exhausted."

When we got home that evening, Harvey was gone to visit with Wheaties and the baby was asleep. Angelina sat me down next to her on the couch. She took my hand and said, "Tell me honestly. Do you want me to work it out with Harvey?"

Here was the truth: "I want you to at least try." If Harvey and Angelina didn't make it, I could be okay with that, but I would have a hard time respecting her if she gave up so quickly, without at least having a fair go of it before just giving up and running off to a new city or jumping into a new relationship. And I wanted to know: "Do you like Maurice?"

Angelina said, "I like him very much. As for anything more—well, that's not an option for us to explore at this moment in time, and we're both respectful of that. And now you owe me a truth. Do you even like Harvey? Because for all that you seem intent on saving our marriage, I've never gotten the impression one way or the other that you were particularly attached to him."

I nodded yes to Angelina's question about me liking Harvey, which was only partially true. I don't have anything particularly *for* Harvey, besides the important fact that he makes me, Wheaties, and Ariel a family, but I don't have anything particularly *against* him either. I don't think I know Harvey well enough to make a fair judgment, for all that we've lived with him for a year. I guess I like him the way I like LA—don't positively love it, but there's potential there and a good history, and I am open to the possibility it could be a permanent part of my life. Or not. But I could potentially feel the same way about Maurice the Australian, but like Angelina said, that's not an option to explore right now.

Angelina said, "Here's another one for you. It's something we don't talk about, but I can't put off this question any longer, much as I'm not sure I want to know the possible answer. Would you prefer to live with Jack?" Angelina's pretty face looked anything but *feel your freshest self* as she waited for my answer.

At first I wanted Jack back in NYC. Then when he said he was moving to LA, I wanted him back in Sydney. Now that he seems to be staying put in LA, I wouldn't mind if he moved back to Penny's starting place, Melbourne. But did I want to live with him permanently? Mostly, I wanted us all to go back to how we were, where I could spend time with each of my parents, who were each doing well in their own lives, wherever they were. I answered, "What I want is for you to work things out so I don't have to make that choice."

Angelina told me that while Bubbe and I were out shopping, she and Harvey had a long talk and they had made their choice: to try. Even though Angelina was loving LA, she planned to return home for the rest of the summer so she and Harvey could see a marriage counselor. They'd agreed to give their marriage at least a few months of counseling before deciding whether to permanently part company, to see if they could work through whatever was wrong.

I told Mom, "I can live with that choice."

I thought about the kind of relationship choices Lucy and Wheaties and Ben and I will have to make when we're adults. When it comes to dating and marriage and all that, I know we won't make the same mistakes as our parents. Ben will be a true-love keeper for me, for sure. Lucy and Wheaties will eventually find their matches, too. Lucy is a babe waiting to be discovered, and I am confident Wheaties will eventually move over to the Hot Dag category for some girl, just not for Lucy (sorry, *boychik*). The only downside is if our core four don't mess up our relationships, then we might not ever have new steps and halves and partners, etc.—and what kind of crazy *tsetumult yiches* (Bubbe's Yiddish-speak for "confused family tree") would that be?

Chapter 23

Lucy

Angus and I were lying on my bottom bunk reading *Aquarium Fishes of the World* when Mum came into my bedroom to retrieve Angus. His bedtime meant protest time, so I asked her to close my door behind them as I really didn't want to hear it. Angus: love you, not your whining. *Mum, it's still light out, bedtime isn't till dark! No, Angus, late July means summer here, not winter—and eight o'clock is bedtime no matter which side of the equator we're on.* I thought the loud bang I heard after Angus left with Mum might be him taking a spiteful knock against the hallway table, but no, there was Annabel at my bedroom window, again.

I raised the window. "Do you not know how to come through a front door?"

Annabel climbed through the window. "Well, family tradition is family tradition. Kind of like the

Who's Your Favorite Dag? game or the new invention of psycho salsa dancing." Once she was standing on the floor, she leaned back over the open window and lifted a suitcase from the ground, brought it through the window, and then placed it on the bottom bunk.

"What's this?" I asked her.

"Mom and Harvey are going back home to New York. They're leaving tomorrow. Things must be going good for Wheaties in Westwood because he chose to stay with his mom and Tia for the rest of the summer. So I was wondering. Is the offer still open for me to share your room if I want to stay in LA the rest of the summer too?"

I said, "Well, if the linen and curtain colors in this room don't have an offensive clashing palette effect to you, seeing as how Mum and I specifically tried to choose Annabel-friendly hues when we first moved from Australia so you would want to stay here with us, then I reckon it's okay."

"You did that for me?" Annabel looked around the bedroom. "You know, the mauve carpet picks up the white and yellow of the flower-patterned linens very well. Good job."

Yes, Princess, we did that a long time ago—nice of you to finally notice!

"I don't know, Miss Picky," I teased. "Those linens might be substandard percale quality. Think you can live with that?"

Annabel smiled. Then she playfully smacked my arm. "Shut up," she said.

"No, you shut up," I said.

She looked more closely inside the bottom-bunk unit. "Is that a picture of Leonardo on the wall? Did you put that there for me?"

"Yeah," I answered. "Like, months ago. Still waiting for your thank you."

Annabel kissed my cheek. "Thank you, Lucy-love," she said, using my Granny Nell's name for me. But then she went over to the wall and ripped off the Leonardo picture, crinkled it, and tossed it into the waste bin. Next she opened her suitcase and took out a rusty old aluminum box. Annabel took several photos of a certain Melbourne footy god out of the box and held them up against the wall. "Which Ben pictures should I put up? All of them?"

I sighed. Time to get the chockies from the kitchen. No sense in wasting any time before celebrating my new roommate. Maybe we could invite Wheaties over to join our festivities. I suspect we're going to have a long but graayate rest of the summer.

By the way, my Aussie accent does not pronounce the word "graayate." It's the bloody Americans who hear it wrong.

About the Author

Rachel Cohn is the author of *The Steps*, the first book about Annabel and Lucy, which *School Library Journal* called "laugh-out-loud funny." She has also written the teen novels *Gingerbread*, its sequel *Shrimp*, and *Pop Princess*. Although she is step free, Rachel does have two wonderful half sisters. She lives in Manhattan.